'Your father forbade you from seeing me and, like a good little Lady Heiress, you jumped when he clicked his fingers.'

'Don't call me that!' Marnie said distractedly, hating the tabloid press's moniker for her.

It wasn't that it was cruelly meant, only that it mistook her natural reserve for something far more grandiose: snobbery. Pretension. Airs and graces. The kind of aristocratic aspirations that Marnie had never fallen in line with despite the value her parents put on them. The values that had been at the root of their disapproval of Nikos.

'So this is revenge?' she murmured, her eyes clashing fiercely with his. Pain lanced through her.

'Yes.'

'A dish best served cold?' She shook her head sadly, dislodging his hand. 'You've waited six years for this.'

'Yes.' Nikos brought his body closer, crushing her with his strong thighs, his broad chest. 'But there will be nothing cold about our marriage.'

Clare Connelly was raised in small-town Australia amongst a family of avid readers. She spent much of her childhood up a tree, Mills & Boon book in hand. Clare is married to her own real-life hero, and they live in a bungalow near the sea with their two children. She is frequently to be found staring into space—a sure-fire sign that she is in the world of her characters. She has a penchant for French food and ice-cold champagne, and Mills & Boon continue to be her favourite ever books. Writing for Modern Romance is a long-held dream. Clare can be contacted via clareconnelly.com or through her Facebook page.

This is Clare's stunning debut
for Mills & Boon Modern Romance—
we hope you enjoy it!

BOUGHT FOR THE BILLIONAIRE'S REVENGE

BY
CLARE CONNELLY

MILLS & BOON

First Published in Great Britain 2017
By Mills & Boon, an imprint of HarperCollins*Publishers*
1 London Bridge Street, London, SE1 9GF

© 2017 Clare Connelly

ISBN: 978-0-263-06950-1

Our policy is to use papers that are natural, renewable and recyclable
products and made from wood grown in sustainable forests. The logging
and manufacturing processes conform to the legal environmental
regulations of the country of origin.

Printed and bound in Great Britain
by CPI Antony Rowe, Chippenham, Wiltshire

BOUGHT FOR THE BILLIONAIRE'S REVENGE

For Dan, my beloved.

PROLOGUE

HIS CAR CHEWED up the miles easily, almost as though the Ferrari sensed his impatience.

He exited the M25, the call he'd received that morning heavy on his mind.

'He's broke, Nik. Not just personally, but his business, too. No more assets to mortgage. Banks are too cautious, anyway. The whole family fortune is going to go down the drain. He's about to lose it all.'

Nikos should have felt overjoyed. There was something about chickens coming home to roost that ought to have brought him amusement. But it hadn't.

Seeing Arthur Kenington suffer had never been his goal.

Using the man's plight to avenge the past, though… *That* idea held infinite appeal.

For six years he'd carried the other man's actions in his chest. Oh, Arthur Kenington wasn't the first elitist snob Nikos had come up against. Being the poorest kid at a prestigious school—'the scholarship boy'—had led to an ever-present sense of being an outsider.

But it had been so much worse with Arthur. After all, the man had paid him to get out of Marnie's life, declaring that Nikos would never be good enough for his precious daughter. Worse, Marnie had listened to her father. She'd dropped him like a hot potato.

Marnie.

Or 'Lady Heiress', as she was known: the beautiful, enigmatic, softly spoken society princess who had, a long time ago, held his heart in her elegant hands. Held it, pummelled it, stabbed it and finally, at her father's behest, rejected it. Thrown it away as though it were an inconsequential item of extremely limited value.

It had hurt like hell at the time, but Nikos had long ago credited it as the fuel that had driven his meteoric rise to the top of the finance world.

A dark smile curved his lips as he navigated the car effortlessly through London's southern boroughs.

The tables had turned; the power was his and he would wield it over Marnie until she realised what a fool she'd been.

He had the power to help her father, to prove his own worth, and finally to hold her heart in his hands and see if he felt like being gentle...or repaying her in kind.

CHAPTER ONE

SHE SHOULDN'T HAVE COME.

The whole way into the city she'd told herself to turn around, go back. It wasn't too late.

But of course it was.

The second Marnie had heard from him the die had been cast. It had fallen into the water of her life, changing stillness to storm within seconds.

Nikos.

Nikos was back.

And he wanted to see her.

The elevator ascended inside the glass building, but it might as well have been plunging her into the depths of hell. A fine bead of perspiration had broken out on her top lip. Marnie didn't wipe it. She hardly even noticed it.

Every cell of her body was focussed on the next half-hour of her life and how she'd get through it.

'I need to see you. It's important.'

His voice hadn't changed at all; his tone still resonated with assuredness. Even at twenty-one, with nothing behind him, Nikos Kyriazis had possessed the same confidence bordering on arrogance that was now his stock in trade. Sure, he had the billions to back it up these days, but even without the dollars in his bank he'd still borne that trademark ability to command.

For the briefest of moments she'd thought of refusing him. So long had passed; what good could come from re-hashing ancient history? Especially when she knew, in the deepest corner of her heart, that she was still so vulnerable to him. So exposed to his appeal.

'It's about your father.'

And the tiny part of Marnie that had wanted to run a mile at the very thought of coming face-to-face with this man again had been silenced instantly.

Her father?

She frowned now, thinking of Arthur Kenington. He'd been different lately. Distracted. He'd lost a little weight, too, and not through any admirable leap into a healthy life-style. She'd become worried, and Nikos's call, completely out of the blue, had underscored those concerns.

The elevator paused, the doors sliding open to allow two men to enter, both dressed in suits. One of them stared at her for a moment too long, in that way people did when they weren't sure exactly where they knew her from. Marnie cleared her throat and looked straight ahead, her wide-set eyes carefully blanked of any emotion. She tried to conceal the embarrassment that always curdled her blood when she realised she'd been recognised.

When the elevator doors swished open to the top floor of the glass and steel monolith at the heart of Canary Wharf, she saw an enormous sign on the wall opposite that pronounced: KYRIAZIS.

Her heart thumped angrily in her chest.

Kyriazis.

Nikos.

'Oh, God,' she whispered under her breath, pausing for a moment to settle her nerves.

The painstakingly developed skill she possessed of hiding her innermost thoughts and feelings from the outside world failed her spectacularly in that moment. Her skin, usually like honey all year round, was pale. Her fingers trembled in a way that wouldn't be stopped.

'Madam? May I help you?'

She blinked, her golden-brown eyes showing turmoil before she suppressed the unwanted emotion. With a smile that sat heavily on her lips, Marnie clicked across the tiled foyer.

More recognition.

'Lady Kenington,' the receptionist said with a small tilt of her head, observing the visitor with undisguised interest from the brown hair with its natural blonde highlights to the symmetrical features set in a dainty face down to the petite frame of this reclusive heiress.

Cold-hearted, the tabloids liked to claim, and to the receptionist there seemed indeed an air of aloofness in the beautiful woman's eyes.

'Yes, hello. I have an appointment with...' There was the smallest hesitation as she steeled herself to say his name aloud to another soul. 'Nikos Kyriazis.'

'Of course.' The receptionist flicked her long red hair over one shoulder and nodded to a banquette of chairs across the room. 'He won't be long. Please, take a seat.'

The anticlimax of the moment might have made Marnie laugh under different circumstances. All morning she'd counted down to this very moment, seeing it as a sort of emotional D-day, and now he was going to keep her waiting?

She moved to the seating area, her lips pursed with disapproval for his lack of punctuality. Behind her there was a spectacular view, framed by a wall of pure glass.

She'd followed his meteoric rise to the top, reading about each success and triumph in the papers alongside the rest of the world. It would have been impossible not to track his astounding emergence onto the world's financial stage. Nikos had built himself into a billionaire with the kind of ease with which most people put on shoes in the morning. Everything he'd touched had turned to gold.

Marnie had contented herself with congratulating him in her dreams. Or reading about him on the internet—except when her heart found it could no longer handle the never-ending assault of images that showed Nikos and *her*. The generic 'Other Woman' he habitually dated. She was always tall, with big breasts, blonde hair and the kind of extroverted confidence that the Marnies of this world could only marvel at.

In a thousand years she'd never be like one of them. Those women with their easy sexuality and relaxed happiness.

As if to emphasise her point, her fingers drifted to the elegant chignon she'd styled her shoulder-length hair into that morning. A few clumps had come loose. She tucked them back into place with care, then replaced her manicured hands in her lap.

Almost twenty minutes later the receptionist crossed the room purposefully. 'Lady Kenington?'

Marnie started, her face lifting expectantly.

'Mr Kyriazis is ready to see you.'

Oh, *was* he? Well, it was about time, she thought crossly as she stood and fell into step behind the other woman.

A pair of frosted glass doors showed a dark, blurred figure that could only be him. The details of his features were not yet visible.

'Lady Kenington, sir,' the receptionist announced.

On the threshold of not just the door but of a moment she'd fantasised about for years, Marnie sucked in a fortifying breath and then, on legs that were trembling lightly, stepped into his palatial office.

Would he be the same?

Would the spark between them still exist?

Or had six years eroded it completely?

'Nikos.'

To her own ears her voice was cool and detached, despite the way her heart was stammering painfully against her ribs. Standing by the windows, he turned to face her at the receptionist's pronouncement, the midafternoon sun casting a pale glow over him that focussed her attention on him as a spotlight might have.

The six years since she'd last seen him had been generous to Nikos. The face she'd loved was much the same, perhaps enhanced by wisdom and the hallmarks of success. Dark eyes, wide-set and rimmed by thick black lashes, a nose that had a bump halfway down from a childhood accident, and a wide mouth set above a chin with a thumbprint-sized cleft. His cheekbones were as pronounced as always, as though the features of his face had been carved from stone at the beginning of time. It was a face that conveyed strength and power—a face that had commanded her love.

He wore his dark hair a little shorter now, but it still brushed his collar at the back and had the luxuriant thickness that had always begged her to run her fingers through it. His dark eyes, so captivating, flashed with an emotion that seemed to Marnie almost mocking.

With pure indolent arrogance he flicked his gaze over her face, then lower, letting it travel slowly across her unimpressive cleavage down to her slim waist. She felt a spike of warmth travel through her abdomen as feelings long ago suppressed slammed against her.

Where his eyes travelled, her skin reacted. She was warm as though he'd touched her, as though he'd glided his fingertips over her body, promising pleasure and satisfaction.

'Marnie.'

Her gut churned. She'd always loved the way he said her name, with the emphasis on the second syllable, like a note from a love song.

The door clicked shut behind her and Marnie had to fight against the instinct to jump like a kitten. Only with the greatest of effort was she able to maintain an impassive expression on her subtly made-up face.

Under normal circumstances Marnie would have done what was expected of her. Even in the most awkward of encounters she could generally muster the basics in small talk. But Nikos was different. *This* was different.

'Well, Nikos?' she said, a tight smile her only concession to social convention. 'You summoned me here. I presume it's not just to stare at me?'

He arched a thick dark brow and her stomach flopped. She'd forgotten just how lethal his looks were in person. And it wasn't just that he was handsome. He was completely vibrant. When he frowned it was as if his whole body echoed the feeling. The same could be said when he smiled or laughed. He was a passionate man who hid nothing. She felt his impatience now, and it burned the little part of her heart that had survived the explosive demise of their relationship.

'Would you like a drink?' His accent was flavoured with cinnamon and pepper: sweet and spicy. Her pulse skittered.

'A drink?' Her lips twisted in an imitation of disapproval. 'At this hour? No. Thank you,' she added as an afterthought.

He shrugged, the bespoke suit straining across his muscled chest. She looked away, heat flashing to the extremities of her limbs. When he began walking towards her, she was powerless to move.

He stopped just a foot or so across the floor, his expression impossible to interpret. His fragrance was an assault on her senses, and the intense masculinity of him was setting her body on fire. Her knees felt as if they might buckle. But although her fingers were fidgeting it was the only betraying gesture of her unease. Her face remained impassive, and her eyes were wide with unspoken challenge.

'You said you needed to speak to me. That it was important.'

'Yes,' he murmured, his gaze once again roaming her face, as though the days, months and years they'd spent separated were a story he could read in it if he looked long enough.

Marnie tried to catalogue the changes that had taken place in her physically in the six years since he'd walked out of Kenington Hall for the last time. Her hair, once long and fair, was shoulder-length and much darker now, with a sort of burnt sugar colour that fell with a fashionable wave to her shoulders. She hadn't worn make-up back then, but now she didn't leave the house without at least a little cosmetic help. That was the wariness she had learned to demonstrate when a scrum of paparazzi was potentially sitting in wait, desperate to capture that next unflattering shot.

'Well?' she asked, her voice a throaty husk.

'What is your rush, *agape mou*?'

She started at the endearment, her fingertips itching as though of their own free will they might slap him. It felt as though a knife had been plunged into her chest.

She flattened the desire to correct him. She needed to stay on point to get through this encounter unscathed. 'You've kept me waiting twenty minutes. I have somewhere else to be after this,' she lied. 'I can't spare much more time. So, whatever you've called me here to say, I suggest you get it over with.'

Again, his brow arched imperiously. His disapproval pleased her in that moment. It eclipsed, all too briefly, other far more seductive thoughts.

'Wherever you've got to be after this, I *suggest* you

cancel it.' He repeated her directive back to her with an insouciant shrug.

'Just as dictatorial as ever,' she said.

His laugh whipped around the room, hitting her hard. 'You used to like that about me, I seem to recall.'

Her heart was racing. She lifted her arms, crossing them over her chest, hoping they might hide the way her body was betraying her. 'I'm definitely not here to walk down memory lane,' she said stiffly.

'You have no idea why you're here.'

She met his gaze, felt flame leaping from one to the other. 'No. You're right. I don't.'

Wishing she'd obeyed her instincts and refused to see him, she began to walk towards the door. Being in the same room as him, feeling the force of his enmity, she knew only that nothing could be important enough to go through this wringer.

Some paths were best unfollowed—their relationship was definitely one of them.

'I don't know why I listened.' She shook her head and her hair loosened a little, dropping a tendril from her temple across her cheek. 'I shouldn't have come.'

He laughed again, following her to the door and pressing the flat of his palm against it. 'Stop.'

She started, and it dawned on him that Marnie was nervous. Her facade was exceptional. Cold, unfeeling, composed. But Marnie was uncertain, too. Her enormous almond-shaped eyes, warm like coffee, flew to his face before she seemed to regain her footing and inject her expression with an air of impatience.

But she *wasn't* impatient. How could she be? The past was claiming her. He was him, and she was her, but they were kids again. Teenagers madly in love, sure of nothing and everything, unable to keep their hands off each other in the passionate way of illicit love affairs.

Sensing her prevarication, he spoke firmly. 'Your father is on the brink of total ruin, and if you don't listen to me he'll be bankrupt within a month.'

She froze, all colour draining from her face. She shook her head slowly from side to side, mumbling something about not being able to believe it, but her mind was shredding through that silly denial. After all, she'd seen for herself the change in him recently. The stress. The anger. The drinking too much. The weight loss. Disturbed sleep. Why hadn't she pushed him harder? Why hadn't she demanded that he or her mother tell her honestly what was going on?

'I have no interest in lying to you,' he said simply. 'Sit down.'

She nodded, her throat thick, as she crossed the room and took a chair at the meeting table. He followed, his eyes not leaving her face as he poured two glasses of water and slid one across the table, before hunkering his large frame into the chair opposite.

His feet brushed hers accidentally beneath the table. The shock of her father's situation had robbed her of her usual control and she jumped at the touch, her whole body resonating before she caught herself in the childish reaction.

And he'd noticed it; the smile of sardonic amusement on his face might have embarrassed her if she hadn't been so completely overcome by concern.

'Dad's…I don't…' She shook her head, resting her hands on the table, trying to make sense of the revelation.

'Your father, like many investors who didn't take adequate precautions, is suffering at the hands of a turbulent market. More fool him.'

He spoke with disrespect and obvious dislike, but Marnie didn't leap to defend Arthur Kenington. At one time she'd been her father's biggest champion, but that, too, had changed over time. Shell shock in the immediate aftermath of Libby's death had translated to the kind of loyalty that didn't allow room for doubt. Her need to keep her family close had made it impossible for her to risk upsetting the only people on earth who understood her grief. She would have done anything to save them further pain, even if that had meant walking away from the man she loved because they'd expressed their bitter disapproval.

Her eyes were cloudy as they settled on his frame. Memories were sharp. She pushed at them angrily, relegating them to the locked box of her mind.

Those memories were of the past. The distant past. She and Nikos were different people now.

'He will lose everything without immediate help. Without money.'

Marnie turned the ring she always wore around her finger—a nervous gesture she'd resorted to without realising. Her face—so beautiful, so ethereally elegant—was crushed, and Nikos felt a hint of pity for her. There was a time when he would have said that causing her pain was anathema to him. A time when he would have leapt in front of a speeding bus to save her life—a time when he had promised to love her for ever, to adore her, to cherish her.

And she'd answered that pledge by telling him he'd never be good enough for her, or words to that effect.

He straightened in the chair, honing in on his resolve.

But Marnie spoke first, her voice quietly insistent. 'Dad has lots of associates. People with money.'

'He needs rather a large sum.'

'He'll find it,' she said with false bravado, unknowingly tilting her gaze down her small ski slope nose.

His smile was almost feral in its confidence. 'A hundred million pounds by the end of the month?'

'A...hundred...' Her feathery lashes closed, muting any visible shock. She was hiding herself from him, wanting to keep her turmoil private and secret.

He didn't challenge her; there was no need.

'And that is just to start,' he confirmed with a small nod. 'But if you want to leave...' He waved a hand towards the door, as though he didn't give a damn what she chose to do.

Marnie toyed with the ring again, her eyes studying its gentle golden crenulations before shifting their focus back to his face. 'So? What's *your* interest in my father's business?'

'His business?' Nikos's laugh was short and sharp. 'I have no interest in that.'

Marnie's eyes knitted together, confusion obvious on her features. Even her hair looked uptight, knotted into that style. Her hands, her nails, her perfectly made-up face: she was the picture of stylish grace, just as her parents had always intended her to be.

'I presume you called me here because you have a plan.' She pinned him with her golden-brown eyes until the sensation overpowered her. 'I wish you'd stop prevaricating and just tell me.'

His smile was not one of happiness. 'You are hardly in a position to issue commands to me.'

Marnie's face lifted to his in surprise. 'That's not what I was doing.' She shook her head timidly from side to side. 'I didn't mean to, anyway. It's just...please. Tell me everything.'

He shrugged. 'Bad decisions. Bad investments. Bad business.' He pressed back further in his chair, the intensity of his fierce gaze sending sharp arrows of awareness and emotion through her blood. 'The why of it doesn't matter.'

'It matters to me.'

He spoke on as though she hadn't. His eyes bored into hers. 'I believe there are not ten people in the world who would find themselves in a financial position to help your father. Even fewer who would have any motivation to do so.'

Marnie bit down on her lower lip, trying desperately to

think of anyone who might have enough liquidity to inject some cash into her father's crumbling empire.

Only one man came to mind, and he was staring at her in a way that was turning her mind to mush.

Unable to sit still for a moment longer, Marnie scraped her chair back and stalked to the window. London vibrated beneath them: a collection of cars and souls all going about their own lives, threading together into one enormous carpet of activity. She felt as if she'd been plucked out of the fibres and placed here instead, in a madhouse.

'Dad's never been your favourite person,' she said softly. 'How do I know you're not making this up for some cruel reason of your own?'

'Your father's demise is not a well-kept secret, *matakia mou*. Anderson told me.'

'Anderson?' The name was like a knife in her gut. She thought of Libby's fiancé with the shock of grief that always accompanied anything to do with her sister. With *Before*.

'We're still in touch,' he said with a shrug, as if that wasn't important.

'He knows about this?' She thought of Anderson Holt's family, the fortune they possessed. Maybe *they* could help? She dismissed the thought instantly. A hundred million pounds—cash—was beyond most people's capabilities. Besides, Arthur Kenington would never let himself be bailed out.

'It is no secret,' Nikos said, misunderstanding her question. 'I imagine the whole city knows the truth of your father's position.'

Her spine stiffened and sorrow for the man who had raised her pushed all thoughts of her late sister's fiancé from her mind. She blinked quickly, denying the sting of tears that was threatening. She was not willing to show such weakness in front of anyone, let alone Nikos.

'He *has* seemed stressed lately,' she conceded awkwardly, keeping her vision focussed on the buzz of activity at street level.

'I can well imagine. The idea of losing his life's work and the legacy of his forebears will be weighing heavily on his conscience. Not to mention his monumental ego.'

She let the barb go by. Her mind was completely absorbed with trying to make sense of this information. 'I don't understand why he wouldn't have said anything.'

'Don't you?' His eyes flashed with anger and resentment as his last conversation with Lord Arthur Kenington came to mind. 'The man prides himself on shielding you from the world. He would do anything to spare you the pain of actually inhabiting reality with the rest of us.'

'You call *this* reality?' she quipped, flicking a disapproving glance around the cavernous glass office decorated with modern art masterpieces and furniture that would have looked at home in a gallery.

A muscle jerked in his cheek and Marnie wished she could pull those words back. Who was *she* to sit in judgement of his success? She didn't know the details, but she knew enough of his childhood to realise that if anyone on earth understood poverty it was Nikos.

'I'm sorry,' she said stiffly, lifting a finger to her temple and rubbing at it. 'None of this is your fault.'

A pang of something a lot like sympathy squeezed in Nikos's gut. Recognising that she could still evoke those emotions in him, he consciously pushed aside any softening towards her.

'No.' He rubbed a hand across his stubbled jaw. 'He stands to lose it all, Marnie. His investments. His reputation. Kenington Hall. He will be a cautionary tale at best, a laughing stock more likely.'

'Don't…' She shivered, thinking of what her parents had already suffered and lost in life. The thought of them enduring yet another tragedy weighed so heavily on her chest she could hardly breathe.

'I would be lying if I said I'm not a little tempted to leave him to his fate. A fate that, as it turns out, is not at all dissimilar to what he predicted for *me*.'

A shiver ran down her spine. 'You're still angry about that?'

His eyes flashed. 'Angry? No. Disgusted? Yes.' He dragged a hand through his hair, as though mentally shaking himself. 'He would spend a lifetime repaying his creditors.'

Nikos was conscious that he was driving a proverbial knife into her. He didn't stop.

'Some of his decisions might even be seen as criminally negligent.'

'Oh, my God, Nikos, *don't*.' She spun to face him; it was like being hit with a sledgehammer.

He ground his teeth, refusing to feel sympathy for her even when her world was shattering. 'It is the truth. Would you prefer I'd said nothing?'

When she spoke her voice was hoarse, momentarily weakened by the strength of her feelings. 'Does this bring you pleasure? Did you bring me here to gloat?'

'To gloat?' His smile was like a wolf's. 'No.'

'Well? Then what *do* you want? Why are you telling me any of this?'

A muscle jerked in his cheek. 'I could alleviate all of your father's problems, you know.'

Hope, a fragile bird, fluttered in her gut. 'Yes?'

'It would not be difficult for me to fix this,' he said with a shrug.

Marnie's head spun at the ease of his declaration. 'Even a hundred million pounds?'

'I am a wealthy man. Do you not read the papers?'

'God, Nikos.' Relief was so palpable that she didn't

even acknowledge the insult. Hope loomed. 'I don't know how to thank you.'

'Delay your gratitude until you have considered the terms.'

'The terms?' Her brows drew together in confusion.

'I have the means to help your father, but not yet the inducement.'

Aware she was parroting, she murmured, 'What inducement?'

The breath burned in her lungs. Her heart was hammering so hard in her chest that she thought it might break free and make a bid for freedom. Tension was a rope, twisting around them. She waited on tenterhooks that seemed to have sharp gnashing teeth.

'You, Marnie.' His dark voice was at its arrogant best. 'As my wife. Marry me and I will help him.'

CHAPTER TWO

She'd never understood how silence could vibrate until that moment. The very air they breathed seemed as if it was alive, crackling and humming around them. His words were little daggers, floating through the atmosphere, jabbing at her heart, her soul, her brain, her mind.

'Marry me and I will help him.'

Only the sound of her heavy breathing perforated the air. For support, she pressed back against the glass window. It was warmed by the sun.

'I don't understand,' she said finally, squeezing her eyes shut. Every fibre of her being instantly rejected the idea.

Or did it?

Briefly, childish fantasies bubbled inside her, spreading the kind of pleasure she'd once revelled in freely.

When she blinked a moment later, Nikos was holding a glass of water just in front of her. She took it and drank gratefully, her throat parched.

'It is not a difficult equation. Marriage to me in exchange for a sum of money that will answer your father's debts.'

'That makes no sense,' she contradicted flatly.

'No?'

'No!'

It seemed like the right reaction. It was an absurd proposal, after all. Wasn't it? She should have felt panicked by the very idea. And perhaps a part of her did. This was the man who had disappeared from her life but never fully from her heart.

But panic and wariness were only tiny components of her emotional tangle. Hope and an intense flare of passionate resonance also filled her.

'Marriage...' Her heart squeezed. Her words were a whisper. 'Marriage...is for people in love. That's not us. How can you be so cavalier about it?'

He took a step closer, curling his fingers around the glass. Instead of taking it from her he kept his hand over hers. Electricity sparked along the length of her arm, shooting blue fire through her body.

'Call it...righting a wrong,' he said darkly, his eyes scanning her face with hard emotion. 'Or repaying a debt.'

Her stomach rolled.

'Your father paid me a considerable sum to get out of your life six years ago.'

Her mouth formed a perfect 'o' and she gasped in surprise. He gathered she hadn't known *that* little piece of information. It didn't make him proud, but he enjoyed seeing her sense of betrayal and outrage before she schooled her features once more. Her mask was excellent, though the more tightly she held on to it the more he wanted to force her to drop it. To shock her, surprise her, make her feel so strongly that she could no longer remain impassive.

He put his thumb-pad over her lower lip, remembering how soft they were to kiss.

'I didn't know.' Her eyes were earnest and it didn't enter his mind to doubt her.

'No.' He shrugged. 'It wasn't necessary, in any event. He obviously didn't realise that you had already conclusively ended things.'

Marnie's heart squeezed. 'I had no choice.'

'Of *course* you had a damned choice.' He controlled his temper with effort. 'You could have told him that you'd fallen in love with me. That no amount of comment about the fact that I didn't live up to his exalted expectations would change how you felt about me. You could have told him to shove his snobbery and his stupidity. You could have fought for what we were—as I would have.'

She sucked in a deep breath. The pain was as fresh in that instant as if it was six years ago. She ached all over. 'You know what we'd been through.' She squeezed her eyes shut. 'What my family had lost. I couldn't hurt him. I had to choose between him and…what I felt for you.'

'And you chose him.' His stare was filled with a startling wave of resentment. 'You switched something in here—' he lifted a finger to her chest, pointing at her heart '—and that was it. It was over.'

She swallowed convulsively. It had been nothing like that. He made it sound easy. As if she'd simply decided to forget Nikos and move on. But she hadn't. She'd agonised over the decision.

She'd tried to explain to her parents that she didn't care that Nikos didn't have money or come from one of the established families they approved of. But arguments had led to the unsupportable—her mother in tears, her father furious and not speaking to Marnie, and the certainty that they just wanted Libby back—perfect Libby—to make good choices and be the daughter they were proud of.

'In any event, the financial…*compensation* for leaving you helped to soften the blow. At first I swore I wouldn't take it. But then…'

He spoke with gravelled inflection, sucking Marnie back to the present.

'I was so angry with you, with him. I took it and I told myself I'd double it—just to prove him wrong. To prove a point.'

Marnie's cheeks were flushed. His hand moved to cup her face. She could have pulled away, but she didn't. 'I think you did more than that.'

His smile was grim. 'Yes.'

So Arthur had given her boyfriend money to get out of her life? A chill ran the length of her spine. It seemed like a step too far. Pressuring her to end it was one thing, but actually forcing Nikos out?

'I'm sorry he got involved like that. It wasn't his place to...to pay you off.'

'Not when you'd already done his bidding,' Nikos responded with a lift of his shoulders. 'Your father forbade you from seeing me and, like a good little Lady Heiress, you jumped when he clicked his fingers.'

'Don't call me that,' she said distractedly, hating the tabloid press's moniker for her.

It wasn't that it was cruelly meant, only that they mistook her natural reserve for something far more grandiose: snobbery. Pretension. Airs and graces. The kind of aristocratic aspirations that Marnie had never fallen in line with despite the value her parents put on them. The values that had been at the root of their disapproval of Nikos.

'So this is revenge?' she murmured, her eyes clashing fiercely with his. Pain lanced through her.

'Yes.'

'A dish best served cold?' She shook her head sadly, dislodging his hand. 'You've waited six years for this.'

'Yes.' He brought his body closer, crushing her with his strong thighs, his broad chest. 'But there will be nothing cold about our marriage.'

Desire lurched through her. The world began to spin wildly off its axis. 'There won't be a marriage,' she said, with a confidence that was completely forged. Already the options were closing in around her. 'And there certainly won't be...what you're...suggesting.'

'What's the matter, *agape mou*? Do you worry that we won't still feel as we did then?'

He ground his hips against her and she groaned as sensations that had long since been relegated to the past flared in her belly. Of their own volition her fingers curled into the fabric of his shirt, the warmth from his chest a balm to her fraught nerves.

'Do you remember how I respected your innocence?' He brought his mouth close to hers, so that his words were a breath on her lips. 'How I told you we should wait until we were married, or at least engaged?'

Shame, desire, misery and despair slid through her like a headless snake, twisting and writhing in her heart. She pulled her lower lip between her teeth and nodded once.

'How, even though I had kissed your body all over, and you had begged me to take you, I insisted that I wanted to wait? Because I thought I loved you and that it mattered.'

He dropped his hands to her hips, holding her still as he pushed against her once more. She tilted her head back as far as she could, the window's glass providing a hard barrier.

'Do you remember how you laughed in my face and told me you'd never marry someone like me?'

Those words! How she'd hated saying them! She'd rehearsed them for days, and when the moment had come only the belief that she was doing the right thing for her family had spurred her on to say them. It was the most difficult thing she'd ever done. Even now, six years later, she wondered at the way she'd been led away from him despite the intensity of her feelings.

'*Do* you?' he demanded, scraping his lips against her neck, sending her pulse rioting out of control.

'Yes!' She groaned as desire and memory weakened her body.

'I have met many people like you in my life—like your father. Snobs who value centuries-old fortune above all else.'

'That isn't me,' she said with quiet determination.

'Of course it is.' He almost laughed. 'You broke up with me because you knew your destiny was to marry someone like you. Somebody that your parents approved of.'

'That's what *they* wanted. I just wanted *you*.'

'Not enough.' He sobered, his mouth a grim slash.

Frustrated, she tried to appeal to the man he'd once been: the man who had known her better than anyone on earth. 'God, Nikos. You *know* what my life was like then. We'd just buried Libby. We were all in mourning. I couldn't upset them like you wanted me to. I *couldn't*. Don't you dare think for a moment it was because I thought you weren't good enough.'

'You thought as your parents wished you to,' he said with coldness, shrugging as though it no longer mattered. 'But they will shortly come to realise there is one thing that carries more sway than birth and breeding. And when you are as broke as your father that is *money*.'

His words fell like bricks against her chest.

'Now you will marry me, and he will have to spend the rest of his life knowing it was *me*—the man he wouldn't have in his house—who was his salvation.'

The sheer fury of his words whipped her like a rope. 'Nikos,' she said, surprised at how calm she could sound in the midst of his stormy declaration. 'He should never have made you feel like that.'

'Your father could have called me every name under the sun for all I cared, *agape*. It was *you* I expected more of.'

She swallowed. Expectations were not new to Marnie. Her parents'. Her sister's. Her own.

'And now you *will* marry me.'

Anticipation formed a cliff's edge and she was tumbling over it, free-falling from a great height. She shook her head, but they both knew it was denial for the sake of it.

'No more waiting,' he intoned darkly, crushing his mouth to hers in a kiss that stole her breath and coloured her soul.

His tongue clashed with hers. It was a kiss of slavish possession, a kiss designed to challenge and disarm. He blew away every defence she had, reminding her that his body had always been able to manipulate hers. A single look had always been enough to make her break out in a cold sweat of need.

'No more waiting.'

'You can't still want me,' she said into his mouth, wrapping her hands around his back. 'You've hardly lived the life of a monk. I would have thought I'd lost all appeal by now.'

'Call it unfinished business,' he responded, breaking the kiss to scrape his lips down her neck, nipping at her shoulder.

She pushed her hips forward, instinctively wanting more. Wanting everything.

Her brain was wrapped in cotton wool, foggy and filled with questions softened by confusion. 'It was six years ago.'

'Yes. And still you're the only woman I have ever believed myself in love with. The only woman I have ever wanted a future with. Once upon a time for love.'

'And now?'

'For...less noble reasons.'

He stepped away, breaking their kiss so easily it made her head spin.

'Your father isn't the only one I intend to prove wrong.'

She narrowed her eyes, her heart racing. 'What does *that* mean?'

His laugh was without humour. 'You said I didn't mean

anything to you. That I had been merely a distraction when you needed to escape grief.'

He brought his face closer to hers once more—so close that she could see the thousands of tiny prisms of light that danced in his eyes.

'You told me you didn't want me.'

'I...' She squeezed her eyes shut. 'I don't remember saying that,' she lied.

'You said it. And I will delight in showing you how wrong you were.'

He stepped away, leaving her cresting a wave of emotion. Striving to sound cool, she said, 'So you've been... what? Pining for me for six years? Give me a break, Nikos. You moved on pretty damned fast, so it's a little disingenuous to be playing the heartbroken ex-lover now.'

'We were never lovers, *agape*.'

Her stomach churned; her cheeks were pink. 'That's not the point I'm making.'

'Whatever point it is you are attempting to make it is irrelevant to me.'

She sucked in an indignant breath but he continued. 'I have not been pining for you. But I *am* an opportunist.' His smile was almost cruel—at least it looked it to Marnie. 'Your father's situation presented me with an opportunity I felt I couldn't resist.'

'Oh, yeah?' she snapped, trying desperately to think of a way out. A way to make him realise how foolhardy this was!

'You will spend every day of our marriage faced with the reality of just how wrong you were.'

Speechless, she fidgeted with her ring, her mind unable to grasp exactly what was going on.

Seemingly he took her silence as a form of agreement. 'A licence can be arranged within fifteen days. I have engaged a wedding planner to oversee the details. Her card is on my desk; take it when you leave.'

She shook her head as the words he was saying tumbled over her. She needed to process what was going on. 'Wait a second. It's too sudden. Too soon.'

He arched a single thick brow. 'Any delay will make it impossible for me to help your father in time.'

'You're saying we have to actually *be* married before you'll help him?'

His lip twisted in a smile of cynical derision. 'It would hardly make sense to prop him up *before* the pleasure of having you... As my wife.'

To Marnie, his slight pause implied that he meant something else altogether. That he wanted to sleep with her before money changed hands. It made her feel instantly dirty, and she shifted away from the window, crossing her arms in an attempt to stem the pain that was perforating her heart.

'Do you think I'd renege on our deal?' she asked, realising only after posing the question that it showed her acquiescence when she hadn't actually intended to agree...*yet*.

'I think you will do whatever pleases you—as you always have done.' His eyes narrowed. 'Forgive me—what is the expression? Having been bitten, I am...?'

'Once bitten, twice shy.' She sucked in an unsteady breath, waiting for relief to calm her lungs. But still they burned painfully. She tried to salvage her pride. 'If I agree to do this, I *will* go through with it.'

'I'm not sure I can put much stock in your assurances,' he said with a shrug. 'I credit you and your father for my scepticism. Were it not for you, perhaps I would have continued to take promises at face value. Now I live and die by contracts.'

'That's fine in business. I'm sure it's wise, in fact. But marriage is different, surely.'

'A *real* marriage,' he conceded, with a tight nod.

'You're saying you don't want ours to be a real marriage?'

His laugh sent a shiver down her spine. 'Oh, in the most important ways it will be.'

'Meaning…?' she challenged—though how could she not understand his intention?

'Meaning, Marnie, that I have no interest in paying a hundred million pounds and tying myself to a woman *purely* for revenge.'

His smile curled her toes.

'There will be other benefits to our marriage.'

Her heart slammed hard in her chest. 'I…' She clamped her mouth shut.

What had she been about to say? That she was still a virgin? That after being so madly in love with him and letting him go she'd found she couldn't feel that same desire for another man? Especially not the men her parents approved of her dating.

'I'm not going to sleep with you just because you appear out of the blue…'

'That is not why you'll sleep with me,' he said.

He spoke with a confidence that infuriated her. But he was right! Despite the passage of time, and the insufferable situation she found herself in, she couldn't deny that the same need was rioting through her now, just as it had in their past.

'This is a deal-breaker,' he said with a shrug. 'These are my terms. Accept them or don't.'

'Wait.' She shook her head and lifted a hand to make him pause for a moment. But she was drowning. Possibilities, questions, wants, needs, doubts were churning around inside her—it was background noise but it was going to suck her under. 'There's so much more to discuss.'

'Such as?' he prompted, crossing his arms over his broad chest.

She tried not to notice the way the fabric strained to reveal his impressive pectoral definition.

'Well, such as...' She darted her tongue out and licked her lower lip. 'Say I went along with this absolutely crazy idea—and I'm not saying I will, because clearly it's madness—where would you see us living?'

'That is also non-negotiable. Greece.'

'Greece?' She was in free fall again. 'Greece, as in... You mean Greece?'

He stared at her for a long moment, his eyes mocking her. 'Athens. My home.'

'But I've always lived *here*. I can't move.'

Their eyes locked; it was a battle of wills and yet when he spoke it was with an easy nonchalance she admired.

'I will be spending a considerable fortune to save your father's reputation. You do not think it's fair that *you* should make some concessions?'

'Marrying you is *not* a c-concession,' she stammered in disbelief. 'It's so much more than that. And the same can be said of moving to a different country.'

'You are *so* sheltered,' he murmured. 'What would you suggest? That we live in London? Within arm's reach of your father? A man I will always despise? No.'

'How can I marry you knowing you feel that way about him?'

His expression was rock-hard. 'You will find a way.' He shrugged. 'While it might be difficult for you, it is the only way to spare him—and your mother—from a considerable fall from grace.'

'So this is how it would be? You'd dictate terms and I'd be expected to fall in with them?'

The air was thick between them. He studied her for a

long moment and she wondered if he wasn't going to answer. Finally, though, he sighed.

'I have no intention of being unreasonable. When you make a fair request I will hear you out. But this is not one of those instances. I live in Greece. My business is primarily controlled from Athens. You still live with your parents, who hate me as much as I do them. You have no business to speak of. It is obvious that we should move.'

'Just like that?' she murmured, shaking her head at his high-handed dictatorial manner even when a small part of her brain could see that he was raising a decent rationale for the suggestion.

'These are my terms,' he said again.

'You're unbelievable,' she replied softly, worrying at her fingers.

She spun her ring some more, trying to think of a way to appease him that didn't involve anything so drastic as this ridiculous marriage. But there was nothing. He had the money. And there was no way he'd help unless she made it worth his while.

'Yes.' He shrugged. 'So?'

'I wouldn't want a big wedding.' She was thinking aloud, really, though to her ears it sounded as though she was going along with his proposal. 'If I had my way it would just be us. No fanfare. No fuss.'

'Hmm…' he murmured with a shake of his head. 'And no one need ever know? No. I want the world to see that you are my wife. You—a woman who once felt I was far beneath her. A woman who declared she'd never marry someone like me. I want your father to have to stand beside us, smiling as though I am all his dreams come true, when we three will know that I am the last man on earth he wants his daughter to marry.'

The way he'd been treated by her and her parents was a nauseating truth. She wished—not for the first time—

that she'd been able to stand up to them. That she'd been wise enough to fight for the relationship that had mattered so much to her.

'Nikos…' She furrowed her brows, searching for words. 'You have to understand why I…why I couldn't be with you. You know how my parents were after Libby…after…'

He studied her face, torn between listening and shutting down this hollow explanation.

'I know I never explained it properly at the time. The way I was always in her shadow. The certainty that I was a poor comparison to her. The absolute blinding fact that they wished again and again that I could be more like her.' She swallowed, an image of her sister clouding her eyes and making her heart ring with nostalgic affection. 'They wanted me to marry someone like Anderson—her fiancé. And I wanted their approval so badly I would have done anything they asked.'

He compressed his lips. 'Yes. I presumed as much at the time.'

He brought his face closer to hers, so she could feel the waves of his resentment.

'You walked away from me and what we were to each other as though I was nothing to you. You can blame your sister, or you can blame your parents, but the only one who made the decision was *you*.'

'I'm trying to explain why…'

'And I'm telling you that it does not matter to me.' His eyes flared. 'You were wrong.'

She had been. In the six years since she'd watched Nikos leave for the last time, his shoulders set, his head held high, she'd never met anyone who excited in her even a tenth of the emotions he had. He alone had been her true love. And she'd burned him in a way that he'd apparently never forgive.

He brought the conversation back to the wedding. 'The guest list will be extensive and the press coverage—'

'Nikos!' Marnie interrupted, her voice strained.

Something in the pale set of her features communicated her distress and he was quiet, watchful.

'Please.' Her throat worked overtime as she tried to relieve her aching mouth. 'I can't do that.'

'You do agree to marry me?'

She nodded. 'But not like that. I... You know how I feel about the media. And, more to the point, how they feel about me.' She flashed a look at him from beneath thick dark lashes. 'I'll marry you. I will. But without all the fuss. Please.'

It was tempting to push her out of her comfort zone. To say that it was a big wedding or none at all. She was staring at him with a look of icy aloofness that had no doubt helped earn her the nickname of Lady Heiress. That look of untouchable elegance bordering on disdain that he understood was her tightly held shield in moments of wrenching panic. That same look he was desperate to dislodge as soon as possible, shaking her into showing her real feelings.

'You don't like the press any more than I do,' she said with measured persistence. 'If you insist on a big wedding we'll both know it's simply to be spiteful to me. And you're not that petty—are you, Nikos?'

He felt his resolve slipping and a grudging admiration for her reasoned argument spread through him. Still, he drawled, 'I'm blackmailing you into my bed and you don't think I'm petty?'

Heat flooded her system, warring with the ice that had coated her heart. 'No, I don't. I think you want me to marry you. What does it matter how we do it?'

She had an excellent point. Besides Marnie there was only one other person he really cared about having at the wedding.

'Fine,' he said, with a nonchalant lift of his shoulders. His eyes glittered with determination. 'So long as your father is there the rest does not greatly matter.'

'It's enormous,' she intoned flatly, rubbing her fingertip over the flattened edges of paper.

Nikos's stare was loaded with emotion. 'It needs to be.' His accent seemed thicker, spicier than it had been the night before. Her gaze flicked to his face, then skidded away again immediately. His face was all angles and planes, unforgiving and unrelenting.

Harsh.

She had never comprehended the full extent of that hardness before. Not in the past, anyway. When she'd loved him as much as the ocean loved the shore. She had felt, then, just like that. As if she would spend the rest of her life rolling inexorably towards him, needing to touch him, to wash over him, to feel him beneath her and around her. She had believed them to be as organically dependent as those two bodies—sea and sand. That without him she would have nowhere to go.

Foolishly, she had thought he felt the same.

But Nikos had moved on quickly, despite his protestations of love, and his bed had been such a hot spot it might as well have had its own listing on TripAdvisor.

'Mind if I have my lawyer check this out?'

He shrugged his shoulders. '*Sígoura.* Certainly. But that may cause a delay to proceedings.'

Her eyes narrowed. 'You mean you might not be able to help Dad in time?'

He sat back in his chair, his body taut, his face unreadable. 'I will not apply for the marriage licence until you have signed the pre-nup.'

A frown formed a little line between her eyes. 'Why not?'

His laugh was a sharp sound in the busy café. A woman

at the table beside them angled her head curiously before going back to her book.

Marnie lowered her voice, not wanting to risk being overheard. She was obliged to lean a little closer. 'Does it matter if I don't sign it in the next week or two? So long as you have it before the wedding...?'

'The minute I apply for our certificate there's a high probability the press will pick up on it. Do you *want* the world to know we were hastily engaged and that the wedding was then cancelled?'

Her cheeks flamed. 'As if the journalists of the world have nothing better to do than search the registry for your name, waiting with bated breath until such time as you see fit to hang up your well-worn bachelor belt,' she muttered.

He arched a single brow, his expression making her feel instantly ridiculous. 'If you believe our wedding won't excite media interest then you're more naive than I recall.'

Yes, she definitely felt childish now. She dragged her lower lip between her teeth, then caught the betraying gesture and mentally shook herself. She was Lady Marnie Kenington, and it was not for Nikos to berate and humiliate her.

'Each of us on our own would create a stir of interest. Marrying one another guarantees press interest.'

'I know.' She nodded. There was no point, after all, in arguing the toss. He was absolutely right. 'But we agreed on a quiet wedding.'

'And I will do my best to arrange this,' he promised.

'Okay.' She nodded again quickly.

His first instinct was to feel impressed by her ability to be reasonable in the face of an argument. But he quickly realised that she wasn't reasonable so much as changeable. That she was deferring to him at the first sign of pressure. Was that how it had been with her parents?

His mouth was a grim line in his face. 'There are four pages you need to sign.'

She expelled a heavy breath and tapped the pen against the side of the table.

Memories, visceral and sharp, twisted his gut. How familiar that tiny gesture was! Flashes of her studying for exams, writing lists, pausing midsentence to capture the next, flashed into his mind. When she'd had a particularly large problem to solve she'd chewed on the end of the pen, waiting for clarity to flood to her from its inky heart.

'Nikos...' She lifted her gaze to him. 'Doesn't this all seem a bit crazy?'

He didn't react.

She huffed out a sigh. 'I don't know you any more. And you definitely don't know me.'

He narrowed his eyes almost imperceptibly. 'I know you perhaps as well as ever.'

She bit on the pen again and shook her head. 'I just don't see why we have to rush this.'

'It is your father's financial situation that puts a time limit on matters.'

'But—'

'No.'

He leaned across the table, pressing his hand on hers. Sparks shimmered in her heart. Angered by her body's ongoing betrayal to his proximity, she worked overtime to conceal the explosive desire. Her glare was dripping with ice.

'This is the only way I will help your father. It's not a negotiation.'

Backed against a wall, she wondered why she didn't feel more angry.

She looked down at the thick pile of papers. 'If you expect me to sign this today then you're going to have to explain it to me.'

'Fine.' He flicked a glance at his gold wristwatch.

'Sorry if I'm taking up too much of your time,' she snapped sarcastically, and for the briefest moment he felt the full force of her emotions—emotions she was so good at guarding. Fear, worry, stress, uncertainty.

But he had no intention of softening towards his fiancée. He nodded curtly, his expression rock-hard. 'The first section deals with our assets. Any assets you bring to the marriage will be quarantined against becoming communal.'

'So I get to keep what's mine?' she interpreted.

'Yes. I have no interest in your money.'

The way he said it, with such vile distaste, made Marnie shiver.

'Fine. Just as I have no interest in yours.'

He arched a brow, his face filled with sardonic amusement. 'You mean, I presume, beyond the hundred million pounds I will be giving your father?'

Her cheeks flamed. 'Yes.' She couldn't meet his eyes because she felt the sting of tears in her own.

'Irrespective of that, you will be entitled to a sum for each year we remain married.'

'I don't want it,' she said through clenched teeth.

'Fine. Give it away. It's not my concern.' He reached forward impatiently and turned several pages until he arrived at the end of that section. 'Sign here.'

Pressing her lips together, she scrawled her name, blinking her eyes furiously.

They were still suspiciously moist when she lifted her face to his. 'Next?'

He appeared not to notice how close her emotions were to the surface. 'The next section deals with the moral obligations of our union. Any infidelity will lead to an immediate termination of the marriage. It will also invalidate the financial agreement, and will necessitate your father returning half of the money I have given him to that date.'

She blinked in confusion. 'You think I'm going to cheat on you?'

His lips compressed with a dark emotion, one she couldn't fathom. 'I could not say with certainty.' His smile was wolfish. 'Though I imagine this makes it considerably less likely.'

She ground her teeth together. 'And what if *you* cheat?'

'Me?' He laughed again, this time with real humour.

'Yeah. You're the one who seems to be constantly auditioning lovers. What happens if you get bored in our marriage and end up in another woman's bed?'

'You will just have to make sure I don't get bored.'

Her breath snagged in her throat. The threat weakened her. Her pulse throbbed painfully in her body. 'When did you get so cynical?'

He narrowed his eyes, stunning her with the heat she felt emanating from him. 'When do you think, *agape mou*?'

She shook her head, hating the implication that she'd somehow caused his character transformation. 'Nikos...'

What did she want to say? She'd already tried to explain about Libby, and the burden she'd felt to please her parents—a burden that had increased monumentally after Libby's death. He didn't care. He'd said as much. She clamped her mouth shut and shook her head. It was futile.

'I have a meeting after this.'

She swallowed, shaking her head to clear the tangle of thoughts. 'Fine.'

'The third section deals with children.'

Her eyes startled to his face. 'Children?' Her heart was jackhammering inside her chest.

He turned several pages but Marnie was too shocked to bother trying to read them. He fixed her with a direct stare. 'It stipulates that we won't have a child for at least five years.'

Fire and ice were flashing within her, making speech

difficult. She blinked her enormous caramel eyes, then shook her head, but still it didn't make sense. 'You want children?'

He shrugged. 'Perhaps. One day. It's hard to imagine right now—and with you.'

'Oh, gee, thanks.' She rolled her eyes in an attempt to hide the way his words had wounded her. 'As if I'm just lining up to be your baby-baker.'

'My...*baby-baker*?' Despite himself, he felt a smile tickle the corner of his lips.

'I can't believe you're actually contracting hypothetical children.'

He arched a brow. 'It makes sense.'

'A baby isn't...' She dropped her gaze. 'A baby isn't *Section Three, Subsection Eleven A*. A baby is a little person. A new life! You have no right to...to...make such arbitrary decisions about something that should be magical and wonderful.'

'A baby between us would *never* be magical and wonderful,' he responded, with such ease that she genuinely believed he hadn't intended to be unkind. 'It is the very last thing I would want. As for it being arbitrary...' He shrugged his broad shoulders with an air of unconcern. 'You seemed perfectly fine making such decisions in the past.'

'Not about a child!'

'You just said you don't want to be my...baby-baker. Have you changed your mind suddenly?' he asked cynically, his eyes drifting over her features with genuine interest.

'No.' She bit down on her lip. The lie—and she recognised it as such—hurt. Images of what their children might look like were hard to shake. Instantly she could see a tiny chubby version of Nikos, with his imperious expression and dark eyes, and her heart seemed to soar at the prospect.

'Our marriage is not one of love. I can think of nothing worse than bringing a child into that situation.'

'But in five years?' she heard herself ask, as if from a long way away.

He shrugged insolently. 'In five years we will either have found a way to live together with a degree of harmony, or we will hate one another and have long since divorced. It gives us time to see what's what. No?'

She nodded jerkily. He was right. She knew he was. But as she signed her name on the bottom of the page she felt as if she was strangling a large part of herself.

'Next?' She forced a tight smile to her lips; her tone was cool.

'A simple confidentiality agreement. Our business is our own. The press has a fascination with you, and I have often thought, despite what you say, that you court their interest.'

'You've got to be kidding me!' she interrupted sharply. 'I go out of my way to stay off their radar.'

'Which in and of itself only heightens their attention and speculation.'

'So I flirt with the press by hiding from them?' She crossed her legs beneath the table. 'That's absurd.'

'You are "Lady Heiress". They call you that because of your behaviour—'

'They call me that,' she interrupted testily, 'because I refuse to engage with them. After Libby died they were everywhere. I was only seventeen, and they followed me around for sport.'

She didn't add how horrible their comparisons to the beautiful Libby had made her feel. How Marnie's far less stunning looks had drawn the press's derision. She had refused to court them in order to create the impression that she didn't care, but each article had eroded a piece of her confidence until only the 'Lady Heiress' construct had remained. Being cold and untouchable, a renowned ice

queen, was better than being the less beautiful, less pop-
ular, less charismatic sister of Lady Elizabeth Kenington.

He shrugged. 'You will not be of such interest in
Greece. Here you are a society princess. There you will
be only my wife.'

Why did that prospect make everything inside her sing?
Not just the prospect of marrying him, but of escaping it
all! The intrusions and invasions. Freedom was a gulf before her.

'Your parents are included in this agreement. They are
to believe our wedding is a real one.'

'Oh? I would have thought you'd like to throw the
terms of our deal in Dad's face, just to see him suffer,'
she couldn't help snapping.

'Perhaps one day.' His smile tilted her world off-bal-
ance. 'But that is *my* decision. Not yours.'

She furrowed her brow. 'This agreement doesn't apply
to you?'

'No. It is a contract for you. So you understand what is
expected of you.'

'That definitely isn't fair.'

He laughed. 'Perhaps not. Do you want to walk away,
Marnie?'

The sting of tears was back. She lowered her eyes in
an attempt to hide them and shook her head. But when
she put her signature to the bottom of the page she added
something unexpected.

A single teardrop rolled down her cheek and splashed
onto the white paper, unconsciously dotting the 'i'. It was
the perfect addition to the deal—almost like a blood promise.

She closed the contract and pushed it across the table.

It was done, then, and there was nothing left to do but
marry the man. Except, of course, to break the news to
her parents.

CHAPTER THREE

'YOU CAN'T BE SERIOUS.' Arthur Kenington's face was a study in apoplexy, from the ruddy cheeks to bloodshot eyes and the spittle forming at the corner of his mouth.

Marnie studied him with a mix of detachment and sadness. Perhaps it was normal to emerge into adulthood with a confusing bundle of feelings towards one's parents. Marnie loved them, of course, but as she sat across from Arthur and Anne in the picture-perfect sunroom of Kenington Hall she couldn't help but feel frustration, too.

She lifted her hand, showing the enormous diamond solitaire that branded her as engaged. Anne's eyes dropped to it; her lips fell at the corners. Just a little. Anne Kenington was far too disciplined with her emotions to react as she wished.

'Since when?' The words were flat. Compressed.

'Be vague on the details.' That had been Nikos's directive when they'd spoken that morning. Had he been checking on her? Worrying she was going to balk at this final hurdle? Did he think the idea of breaking the news to her parents might be too difficult?

'We met up again recently. It all happened very fast.'

'You can certainly say that.' Anne's eyes, so like Libby's had been, except without the warmth and laughter, dropped to Marnie's stomach. 'Is it...?'

'Of course not!' Marnie read between the lines. 'I'm not pregnant. That's not why we're getting married.'

Arthur expelled a loud breath and stood. Despite the fact it was just midday, he moved towards the dumb waiter and loudly removed the top from a decanter of sherry. He poured a stiff measure and cradled it in his long, slim fingers.

'Then why the rush?' Anne pushed, looking from her husband to her daughter and trying desperately to make sense of the announcement that was still hanging in the air.

'Be vague on the details.'

'Why not?' she murmured. 'Neither of us wants a big wedding.' She shrugged her slender shoulders, striving to appear nonchalant even when her heart was pounding at the very idea of marriage to Nikos Kyriazis.

'Darling, it's not how things are *done*,' Anne said with a shake of her head.

Marnie stiffened her spine imperceptibly, squaring her shoulders. 'I appreciate that your preference might be for a big, fancy wedding, but the last thing I want is a couture gown and a photographer from *OK! Magazine* breathing down my back.'

Anne arched one perfectly shaped brow, clasped her hands neatly in her lap. At one time, not that long ago, Marnie might have taken Anne's displeasure as reason enough to abandon her plans. But too much was at stake now. If only her parents knew that the wedding they were so quick to disapprove of was their only hope of avoiding financial ruination!

'You don't like the press. That's fine. But our friends. Your family. Your godmother…!'

'No.' Marnie didn't flinch; her eyes were tethered to her mother's. 'That's not going to happen. Just you and Dad.'

'And Nikos? Which of *his* family will be there?' Anne couldn't quite keep the sneer from her voice.

'As you know, he has no family,' Marnie responded with a quiet dignity. 'Besides me.'

How strange it was to say that, knowing it was the literal truth if not a particularly honest representation of the situation.

'I don't like it,' Arthur interjected, his sherry glass empty now, and his focus on Marnie once more.

Marnie had expected this, and yet still she heard the words with an element of disappointment. 'Why not?' she queried quietly.

'I have never thought he was right for you. I still don't.'

There was nothing inherently offensive in the statement, but it was the reasoning behind it that Marnie took exception to. Six years ago she'd let the implication hang in the air, but now she was older and wiser and significantly less worried about upsetting her parents. 'For what reason, Dad?'

He reached for the sherry once more and Anne Kenington, across from Marnie, stiffened visibly.

'He's just not *right*.'

'That's not a reason.' Marnie's smile was forced.

'Fine. He's different. From you. From us.'

'Because he's Greek?' she asked with an assumption of mock innocence.

'Don't be obtuse,' he snapped.

Anne stood, moving her slender figure across the room towards the large glass doors that opened out onto the rolling green grass of the East Lawn. A large oak broke up the expanse of colour a little way in the distance, casting dark shadows beneath its voluminous branches.

'Is there any point in having this discussion?' she asked wearily.

'Meaning…?' Marnie asked softly.

'Your plans appear to be set in stone,' Anne continued, her pale eyes skimming over the gardens, her face a mask of calm despite the storm Marnie knew to be raging beneath.

Was that the only thing they had in common? Their steadfast commitment to burying any display of emotion? Keeping as much of themselves as possible hidden from prying eyes?

Marnie shifted her gaze back to her father. He looked as if he was about to pop a blood vessel. He was glaring at the sherry decanter, his fingers white around the fine crystal glass.

'One hundred per cent.' Marnie nodded. 'I hope you can put the past behind you and be happy for us.'

Arthur's harsh intake of breath was smothered by Anne's rushed statement. 'You're a grown woman. Who you marry is your choice.' She practically coughed on the statement.

Marnie stood, not sure what else she could add to the conversation. 'Thank you.'

A ridiculous way to end the conversation but, then again, what about the circumstances of this wedding *wasn't* ridiculous?

She slipped from the room, the muted voices of Arthur and Anne chasing her down the long corridors of Kenington Hall. She emerged onto the front steps and breathed in deep. Her cheeks were flushed, her skin warm. She moved deliberately away from the East Lawn, wanting to be far from her parents.

She walked with innate elegance until she reached the edge of the rose gardens. Then she slipped her pumps from her feet and cast one last glance towards the house. She began to move as she'd wanted to since she'd first seen Nikos again. As though the earth had turned to magma and was burning through the soles of her feet. She couldn't stand still; she could no longer be composed and calm.

And so she ran.

She ran as though the ghosts of the past had taken animal form: they were lions and tigers and they were chasing her, making her tremble with fear and terror.

'No daughter of mine is going to throw her life away on a no-hoper like that! You will end it, Marnie, or you will be out of this house faster than you can say inheritance.'

Arthur's hateful declaration was a cheetah, fierce and gnashing its teeth.

'I don't care about money! I love him!'

She sobbed as she remembered her impassioned cry, her belief that if she could only get her parents to understand what a good man Nikos was they would shelve their dislike.

But their dislike hadn't had a lot to do with the man he was so much as the man he *wasn't*.

'He's got no class. He will never make you happy, darling.'

At least Anne had tried to couch her objections gently. But her meaning had been clear. No class. No money. No social prestige.

Even then she'd stood fast. She'd fought for him.

'We've been through enough this year, for God's sake!' Arthur had finally shouted. *'We've already lost one daughter. Are you going to make us lose you, too?'*

Marnie ran until her lungs burned and her eyes stung with the tears the wind held in check. She ran past the lake that she'd fallen into as a child, before she'd learned to love the water and to navigate its murky pull; she ran around the remnants of the tree house where she and Libby had spent several long, sticky summers, pretending they were anywhere but Kenington Hall. She ran to the very edges of the estate, where an apple orchard shielded the property from the curious view of a passer-by.

Finally she came to an abrupt stop beneath a particularly established tree, bracing her palm against the trunk and staring back at the sprawling stone mansion.

Her whole life had been lived within its walls. She'd learned to walk, she'd played hide-and-seek, she'd read book after book, she'd been a princess in a castle. It was her place in the world.

But why hadn't she left when her parents had taken a stand against Nikos? Why hadn't she moved to London like most of her friends?

Because of Libby.

A sob clogged her throat. She swallowed it.

They'd lost Libby. And it had changed them for ever. Maybe they would have been difficult and elitist, anyway. But their grief had made it worse. And it had made Marnie more forgiving.

How could she run away from them and leave them alone after burying one of their daughters?

She groaned now, shaking her head.

So she'd put her life on hold. She'd remained at home, under their roof, managing the gardens, working in her little home office, pretending she didn't resent them for their heavy-handed involvement in a relationship that had been so important to her.

Was this marriage to Nikos a second chance? Might they even fall in love again?

Her heart turned over in her chest as she remembered the exquisite emotions he had evoked in her as a teenager. She had loved him fiercely then—but not enough. Because she'd walked away from him instead of staying and fighting and there was no turning back from that.

Goose bumps danced along her soft skin. 'This is beautiful.'

And it was. The house was nothing like she'd imagined. Set high on a hill on the outskirts of Athens, it was crisp white against a perfect blue sky. Geraniums tumbled out of window boxes, creating the impression that the flowers had sprung to life there and decided to blow happily in the light, balmy breeze. Clumps of lavender stood proud from large ceramic pots and the fragrance of orange blossom and jasmine hung heavy in the air.

'I'll give you a tour tomorrow—introduce you to the household staff.'

'Staff?' That was interesting. 'How many staff?'

He put his hand in the small of her back, propelling her gently towards the front door. 'My housekeeper, Eléni, and her husband, Andréas. Two gardeners...'

'That's good,' she said with a nod.

His laugh was a short, sharp bark. 'Did you think it would be just you and me?'

Of course she had.

He leaned closer, so that she could see the hundred and one colours that danced in his irises.

'Don't worry, *agape mou.*'

The heat of his words fanned her cheek.

'They will give us plenty of space in the beginning. We *are* on our honeymoon, after all.'

Her stomach lurched. Desire was swarming over her body, making her pulse hammer. Moist heat slicked through her. It felt as if she'd been waiting an eternity to be possessed by this man. The time was almost upon them, and anticipation was flicking delicious little sparks over her nerves.

He pushed the front door inwards. A wide tiled corridor led all the way to glass doors that showed the moonlit Aegean Sea in the distance.

'Are you hungry?'

Despite the fact that it was their wedding day, she hadn't eaten more than a piece of wedding cake after the ceremony. A sip of champagne to wash it down and Nikos had whisked her away from the disapprovingly tight smiles of her parents.

Her stomach made a little growl of complaint. 'Apparently,' she said, with an embarrassed smile.

His smile was the closest thing to genuine she'd seen on his face. It instantly offered her a hint of reprieve.

'There is food in the fridge. Come.'

She fell into step behind him, taking in the blur of their surroundings as she walked at his pace. Beautiful modern artwork gave much-needed colour to a palette of all glass and white. The home was obviously new, and it was a testament to minimalist architecture. While beautiful, it was severely lacking in comfortable, homely touches.

The kitchen housed a large stainless steel fridge. He reached in and pulled out a platter overflowing with olives, cheese, bread, tomato and *dolmades*. Another selection of bread was complemented with sliced meats and smoked fish.

'Wine, Mrs Kyriazis?'

The name splintered through her heart. 'I thought I'd keep Kenington,' she said, though in truth she'd barely contemplated the matter.

He poured two glasses of a pale, buttery-coloured wine, his face carefully blank of emotion. 'Did you?'

She shrugged. 'Lots of women do, you know.'

He nodded thoughtfully. 'But you are not "lots of women". You are my wife.'

He said it with such a sense of dark ownership that she was startled. Marnie couldn't have said if it was surprise at being spoken of almost as an object that inspired her sense of caution, or the fact that his passionate statement of intent was flooding her with desire and overarching need. A need that made rational thought completely impossible.

She sipped her wine in an attempt to cool the fire that was ravaging her central nervous system. It didn't work.

She nodded jerkily, at a loss for words.

'I want the world to know it.'

The statement hung between them like a challenge.

Her stare was direct. 'I'm not planning on hiding my identity.'

He reached for a cube of feta and lifted it towards her lips. Surprised, she parted them and he slid the cheese into her mouth, watching with satisfaction as she chewed it.

'No.' His eyes bored into hers, holding her gaze for several long, fraught seconds. 'My wife will bear my name.'

There it was again! That flash of pleasure in her abdomen. A sense of *rightness* at the way he wanted to claim her. To possess her. The desire to subjugate herself completely to his will terrified her. She bucked against it even as she wanted to move to him and offer her submission.

'Will she, now?' she murmured.

'Of course it is not too late to back out of this agreement.' He shrugged. 'Our marriage could be easily dissolved at this point, and I have not yet spoken to your father about his business concerns.'

Something lurched inside her. She stared across at him, needing her wine to banish the kaleidoscope of butterflies that were panicking, beating their wings against the walls of her stomach.

'Are you going to threaten me whenever I don't let you have your way?'

His laugh was without humour. 'That was not a threat, Mrs Kyriazis. It was a summation of our current circumstances.'

'So if I don't take your name you'll divorce me?'

His lips twisted in a wry smile. 'At this point I believe we could simply seek an annulment.'

'You should have put it in that damned pre-nup,' she said with a flick of her lips.

Anger flared inside her and beneath the table she turned the ring on her finger, looking for comfort and relief.

'I would have if I had known you were going to be so irrational about such trivialities.'

'It's not a triviality!' she demurred angrily, tipping more wine into her mouth.

How could she possibly explain her feelings? Explain how essential it was to hold on to at least a part of her identity? How terrified she was that she was married to a man who despised her, who was using her to avenge an ancient rebuff, who was determined not to care for her—a man she had always loved?

'You are my wife.'

'And taking your name is the *only* way to be your wife?' She had to force herself not to yell.

'Not the only way, no.'

His teeth were bared in a smile that sent shivers down her spine. Need spiked in her gut. She wouldn't acknowledge it. She couldn't.

'Fine.' She angled her head away. 'Whatever. I don't care enough to fight about it.'

That bothered him far more than the suggestion she might not take his name. The way she'd rolled over, acquiesced to his wishes at the first sign of conflict. Just like the last time he'd challenged her and she'd almost immediately backed down.

Arthur and Anne had insisted she couldn't be involved with him. Had she argued calmly for a moment and then given up? Given *him* up, and with him their future? Had they invoked her dead sister, knowing that Marnie had never felt she measured up to St Libby? Had they compared him—a poor Greek boy—to Libby's blue-blood fiancé, with his title and his properties? Had she looked from Nikos to Anderson and agreed that, yes, she needed someone like the latter?

'These olives are delicious,' she said quietly, anxious to break the awkward silence that was heavy in the room.

But when she lifted her gaze slowly to his face she saw he was lost in thought, staring out of the kitchen windows at the moonlit garden. It allowed her a moment to study his face and see him properly. He looked tired. No, not *tired*, exactly, she corrected, so much as…what? What *was* the emotion flitting across his face? What did she see in the tightening of his lips and the darkening along his cheekbones? In the knitting of his brow and the small pulsing of that muscle in his jaw?

'Fine.' He blinked and turned to face her. 'I'll show you the house now.'

She nodded out of habit.

It was enormous, and modern throughout. Wide corridors, white walls, beautiful art, elegant lighting…

'It's like a boutique,' she murmured to herself as they finished their tour of the downstairs rooms and took the stairs to the next level.

'This will be our room.' He paused on the threshold, inviting her silently to precede him.

Our room. Did he expect her to argue over their sleeping arrangements? She had no intention of giving him the pleasure.

'It's very nice.' Her almond-shaped eyes skimmed the room, taking in the luxurious appointments almost as an afterthought. King-size bed, bay window with a small seat carved into the nook, plush cream carpet and a door that she imagined led to a wardrobe.

She spun round, surprised to find him standing right behind her. They were so close her arms were brushing his sides.

She stepped back jerkily. 'I'm going to need an office space.'

'An office space?' His laugh was laced with disbelief and it irked her to the extreme.

'Yes. Why do you find that funny?'

'Well, *agape*, offices are generally for *work*.'

'Oh, I see.' She nodded with mocking apology. 'Work like *you* do, I suppose you mean?'

He crossed his arms over his chest, drawing Marnie's attention to the impressive span of musculature.

'Yes, generally.'

Her temper snapped, but she didn't show it. She'd had a lot of practice in keeping her deepest feelings hidden—she could only be grateful for that now.

'I need an office.' She said the words slowly and with crisp enunciation. 'For *my* work.'

'What work?'

Curiosity flared in his gut. Six years had passed and he'd presumed she was still simply Lady Marnie Kenington, daughter of Lord and Lady Kenington, employed only in the swanning about of her estate, the beautifying of herself and the upholding of the family name. It had never occurred to him that she might have done what most people did and found gainful employment. Frankly, he was surprised her parents had approved such a pedestrian pursuit.

'Does it matter? Do you care? Or are you just surprised that I haven't been rocking in a corner over the demise of our relationship since you left?'

Though frustrated by her reticence to speak honestly, he liked seeing the spark that brought colour to her cheeks and impishness to her eyes.

It intrigued him. He far preferred it to the obedient contrition she'd modelled in the kitchen. Instantly he thought of other ways in which he might inspire a similar reaction.

He nodded, concealing his innermost thoughts. 'Fine, have it your way. I do not need to know about your employment if you do not wish to speak of it.' He shrugged, as though the conversation was now boring him. 'I'll have a room made available. Just let my assistant know what you need in terms of infrastructure and he'll see you're set up.'

'*He?* You have a male assistant?'

It was Nikos's turn to act surprised. 'Yes. Bart. He's been with me five years.'

She laughed quietly and shook her head. 'I guess that makes sense. I can imagine you'd run through female secretaries pretty damned fast, given your track record for taking any woman with a pulse to bed.'

'Jealous, *agape*?'

She'd been jealous, all right. For years she'd followed his exploits in the gossip columns. Like watching a train crash, she'd been powerless not to stare at the pictures. They'd come to life in her over-fertile imagination so that she hadn't simply looked at an attractive couple coming out of some hot spot so much as imagined them in bed, or perhaps on the dining table, or the kitchen floor, while *she* lay in her own bed. Alone, untouched, able only to dream of Nikos rather than feel his hands on her body...

'Oh, yes,' she simpered, with an attempt at false sincerity. 'I've spent the last six years *desperately* waiting for you to reappear in my life. I've been missing you and dreaming about you and praying you'd turn up and blackmail me into a loveless marriage. This is pretty much the high point of my life, actually.'

'And we haven't even slept together yet,' he said, in a voice that was honey and dynamite.

Her breath caught in her throat. She spun away from him, her cheeks flushed.

'What is it, *agape*? Suddenly you are shy? It is our wedding night.'

She lifted a hand to her throat and lightly rubbed her skin. 'I... Of course not.' She squared her shoulders.

Hadn't she been dreaming about this for as long as she'd known him?'

'Relax.' His hands on her shoulders were firm. He spun her in the circle of his arms so that they were facing one another, his warmth offering some comfort to her. 'You are shaking like a leaf.'

Tell him the truth!

She fluttered her eyes closed, her lashes dark circles against her pale cheeks.

'You are my wife.' He pressed a finger under her chin, lifting her face to his. His eyes were troubled, tormented. 'Are you...*afraid* of me?'

It was so uncharacteristic of him to show doubt that she raced to reassure him. 'Of course I'm not.' She shook her head, inhaling a deep breath that flooded her system with his spicy scent. 'I'm afraid of *myself*, and of what I want right now.'

He nodded, silently imploring her to continue.

'You hate my father. I think you might even hate me.' She lifted a finger to his lips to stop him from speaking. 'But I don't hate you.' Her eyes were enormous, loaded with fear and desire. 'I don't hate you...'

Her finger, initially placed against his mouth to silence him, dragged slowly across his lower lip. Her eyes followed its progress as if mesmerised.

She knew he was going to kiss her. The intent was in every line of his body. If she'd wanted to she could have stepped away. She could have asked for more time. Instead she lifted herself up on tiptoe, crushing her mouth to his.

In that bittersweet moment all Marnie needed was to right one of the biggest wrongs of her past: she wanted Nikos and, damn it, she was finally going to have him.

To hell with the consequences. They'd be waiting for her afterwards.

CHAPTER FOUR

HER BODY FLASHED like flame when his mouth crushed down on hers with the kind of intensity that spoke of long-held desire. She was powerless to swim against the tide of need: powerless and unwilling.

Her feminine heart was hot and wet, slick with moisture and need. Unfamiliar but instinct-driven urges were controlling her body. Her hands pushed under his shirt, seeking skin and warmth. She traced her fingertips up his hair-roughened chest, splaying her fingers wide. She felt the beating of his heart beneath her touch; it was as frantic as her own.

His body weight pushed her downwards—not to the bed but to the floor, to her knees. He knelt with her, kissing her, his tongue clashing fiercely with hers as his hands pulled through her hair then pushed at her head, holding her against his mouth. She groaned into him, marking their kiss with the desperation that was scrawling a painful tattoo across her being—inking her as his in a way that would never be erased.

He pulled at her as his body pushed at hers until she fell back onto the carpet. His weight on top of her was divine. She curved her hands to his back, digging her nails into his warm skin as she felt the power of his arousal for herself. Hard and firm through their layers of clothing, A bodily ache was spreading through her. She lifted her hips, silently begging him for more. To mark her once and for all.

'Nikos!' She cried his name into the room and he groaned in response. 'Please!' She dug her hands inside his jeans, cupping the naked curve of his arse, pressing him against her and grinding herself intimately against his masculinity.

He laughed throatily. 'You want this, huh?'

He kissed her again—hard, fiercely, possessively—and then roamed his lips lower, encircling one of her erect nipples through the fabric of her dress and her bra. Even with such obstacles in the way the warmth and pressure of his mouth sent sharp arrows of need spiralling within her.

'Yes!' she hissed, arching her back, desperately needing more. 'Please, please...'

'In time.'

He smiled, running his mouth lower, over the fabric of her dress, until he reached the apex of her thighs. He skimmed lower, to the hem of the dress, and finally pushed it upwards, so that only a flimsy scrap of lace stood between him and her most intimate flesh.

Her cheeks were pink, her eyes fevered. Even when he wanted to go quickly he took his time, removing her underpants, sliding them down her soft, smooth legs and discarding them to one side. He let his hands dance patterns along her thighs, revelling in the way she quivered beneath his touch as her body responded instantly to him.

His fingers worshipped at her crease, teasing her, exploring her, aching for her. He was more gentle than he'd known he could be, perhaps afraid that she might regret her decision at any moment. That after years of waiting this was, after all, *not* to be.

Greek words, whispered hoarsely, filled the air. Words that swirled around her, wrapping her in magic and myth.

She didn't have a clue what he was saying, but she loved the sound of his native language.

When he slid a finger into her core she bucked hard, writhing at the intimate touch. Even back then, when they'd been fevered and passionate, he hadn't passed *this* threshold. His invasion was completely, utterly unprecedented.

Sharp, hot barbs of pleasure drove through her body, into her mind, weakening every earthly thought before it could be imagined. He moved slowly, curiously, watching her face as he stroked her sensitive flesh, learning what made her almost incandescent with desire before pulling out of her.

She gasped, the withdrawal of his touch an unbearable pain she could not withstand. But he didn't leave her for long before dropping his lips to her opening. His tongue was warm, but she was more so. Her body was on fire... his mouth seemed to kiss flame into her.

It had been a long time since Marnie had felt anything like this. She was completely unprepared for the insanity that his ministrations would bring. She was digging her nails into the carpet at her sides now, her knees lifted towards the ceiling as her toes curled into the ground and her whole body shook and quivered.

The orgasm was intense. She screamed as it saturated her being in long, luxuriant waves.

Sweat beaded her brow; heat painted her cheeks pink. Her throat, her arms—she was burning up. Her breath was loud in the room as she panted, satiated passion making her lungs work overtime.

Before she could drift down from the clouds that had absorbed her into their heavenly orbit Nikos was straddling her, his arousal pressed against her tingling core.

Marnie stared up at him, and everything in her world was perfect.

He studied her as his hands worked the buttons of his

shirt, and she was powerless to look away. Her tongue darted out, licking her lower lip, moistening it hungrily.

His smile was sexy as sin. She groaned, impatient for more. As he pushed at his shirt her trembling fingers unfastened his belt and pulled it from his jeans. She cast it across the room, wincing apologetically when it hit the wall loudly. He didn't react.

His shirt was unbuttoned, his chest exposed to her greedy eyes, and she stared and she touched and she felt, tracing his muscles, circling his nipples and filling with pride when he sucked in a raspy breath. He rotated his hips, taking back the upper hand, making her weak with the promise of what was to come.

She pushed at his shirt, chasing it down his arms, catching the fingers of one hand as she passed, lifting it to her lips and kissing him. It was a tender moment in the midst of passion. Their eyes locked and the past was all around them, threatening to suck them into the vortex of what had been.

'It might have cost me a small fortune, but finally you are going to be mine.'

His eyes glittered with dark anger, and the moment was swallowed up by cruelty as though it had never been.

Marnie bit down on her lip, trying not to react, trying not to let the pain sour what they were sharing.

She didn't have long to absorb his words, to turn them over in her mind. He shifted his body weight so that he could kick his jeans and boxers off. He was naked. Gloriously, wonderfully naked. She stared at him, her mind disappearing completely at the sight of Nikos Kyriazis. Her husband: the definition of tall, dark and sexy.

She groaned, dropping her hand to her womanhood, her fingers lightly grazing her flesh. His chest heaved as he sucked in a breath, his eyes sparking with hers. He stood over her, incapable of looking anywhere but at her hand and incapable of moving.

Until something snapped—and a desperate need to finally possess her cracked through him.

'You're on the pill.'

It was a statement, not a question. As though it hadn't occurred to him in earnest that she might not be.

Her cheeks flushed pink as she nodded. It had been the first thing she'd done after signing the pre-nuptial agreement. It had been all she could do to prepare for this moment, for him.

'I am safe.'

He straddled her, almost trapping her hand, but she snaked it higher. Tentatively, nervously, as though she had no right, she touched his length. He jerked instantly in her palm. She smiled a feminine, feline smile of innate power.

'You?'

'Me...?' He was long and smooth and so, so hard.

He laughed throatily. 'You've been tested?'

'Oh.' She hadn't been but, having never shared her body with another, she supposed it was the same thing. 'I'm safe, yes.'

He kissed her mouth, squashing her hand, his flesh against her stomach. 'Good. Because I want to feel you, *agape. Really* feel you.'

He jerked out of her grip, bringing his tip to her opening, teasing her with his nearness before pulling away. His hands pushed her dress higher, so that he could lift her breasts out of her bra, rub his palms over her flesh. He pushed the dress roughly over her body, the fabric grazing against her over-sensitised skin, pushed it over her face. She shifted upwards so that he could lift it and toss it. Her bra was next.

She opened her mouth, knowing she didn't want to surprise him with her virginity. She had no sexual experience, but even *she* thought it was somehow not good etiquette to spring that on someone.

But his mouth took hers, making speech impossible, driving rational thought from her brain once more. She tried to cling on to her conviction, to the knowledge that she should speak the truth to Nikos, but it was like chasing a piece of shell in eggwhite.

It slipped out of her mind. Only the physical remained.

His hands were insistent on her breasts, his thumb and forefinger teasing her nipples, rolling them, before his mouth dragged down her throat to take a peach areola into his mouth. His tongue lashed it and she groaned, felt pleasure building to another inevitable crescendo.

Her heart hammered against her ribs, so hard and fast she could hear the pounding of it in her ears.

She lifted her legs, wrapping them around his waist, pulling him closer. He groaned, his stubble-roughened chin like sandpaper on her soft flesh as he moved his mouth to her other breast, delighting it with the same treatment. His tongue lashed her, chasing invisible circles around the erect peak until she could bear it no longer.

'Nikos!' she cried out, tightening her grip around his waist. 'Please, please now…'

He laughed, but it was a sound without humour. 'I thought we'd at least get to bed,' he said ruefully, bringing his tip closer.

There was no fear for Marnie. Despite her innocence, and his impressive size, she knew that this coming together was somehow destined. She had waited a long time for him, and she wasn't about to let something as silly as fear or concern take the shine off the moment.

Still… That explanation she owed him…the warning…

'Nikos, I need to tell you—'

'No.' He pinned her with his gaze as he lifted himself

up on his arms so that he could stare into her eyes. 'No more explanations. No more words. Not now.'

'But—'

'This is not the time for conversation.'

She might have argued with him. After all, she had a strong sense that it was an important thing to share. But before she could say another word he parted her legs, pressing them back onto the carpet, splaying them wide, and thrust into her.

Not gently, nor slowly—why would he?

They were at a fever pitch of desire and he had no reason to suspect that everything they were doing was new and therefore held the potential for pain.

Her eyes squeezed shut as he slammed past the invisible barrier of her innocence, discarding it as swiftly and easily as he had her bra. He swore, the harsh sound jarring her nerves, then swapped to Greek and released a litany of words in his own tongue.

The pain, which had been sharp and searing, was quick to vanish. Like a receding shoreline it disappeared, leaving only the surrender to pleasure in its wake. She moaned as her muscles stretched to welcome him, squeezing his length, gripping him at her core.

He swore again and then shifted, moving gently now, slowly, his eyes on her face, watching for any sign of discomfort. There was none. She began to moan as he stoked her fires. His lips claimed hers, his tongue duelling with hers in time with each delicious thrust until she was about to explode. She curled her toes into the carpet and cried out, the sound muffled by his mouth.

She was incapable of controlling the sensation of release. It burst from her through every pore, every nerve ending. It flew from her body like a bubble being released underwater. It burst, spilling her pleasure across the room in an effervescence of cries and hard breathing.

She arched her back in an ancient step in the dance of sensuality. He gripped her hips, holding her there, his fingers digging into her flesh. He pressed his forehead to hers, their sweat mingling.

He didn't let her catch her breath before he was torturing her anew. Nerve endings already vibrating at an almost unbearable frequency began to quake and quiver. She groaned as another orgasm, bigger and scarier, chased the other away. This time, though, when she cried out into the room, he chased after her, his own voice combining with hers as pleasure saturated their surroundings.

It was a perfect moment.

Marnie caught the pearl of memory—the way he felt, smelled, tasted—and wrapped it deep into the recesses of her mind, knowing she would want to visit this feeling again and again and again.

He lifted up from her, and the absence of his weight was a pain she hadn't been prepared for. He pulled away, removing himself from her heart and standing in one swift movement. He paced away, gloriously naked, and for the briefest moment Marnie thought he was actually going to stalk out of the room without a word!

Incensed, she got to her feet, wincing as muscles that had never been tested began to groan in complaint. The sound of running water heaped fuel onto the fire of her anger. He was actually going to shower straight away? Hell, she had no point of reference, but Marnie would have put money on that being an absolutely hurtful thing to do.

The door she had initially thought was a wardrobe must conceal an *en-suite* bathroom.

The shower was running when she stepped into the tiled room, but Nikos was not behind the glass. He stood, naked, his hands braced on the vanity unit, his head bent. She couldn't see his expression in the mirror, but tension seemed to emanate from his strong frame.

It arrested her in her tracks.

Fear that she'd somehow got something wrong swirled through her.

She cleared her throat, uncertain what she wanted him to say but knowing she needed to hear *something*. Some form of reassurance or kindness.

He lifted his head, his eyes spearing hers in the mirror's reflection. His face was strained, his expression otherwise unreadable. He scanned her face, seeming to shake himself out of his own reverie, then turned to look at her.

'Did I hurt you?'

It was so far from what she'd expected him to say that relief whooshed through her. She shook her head wordlessly.

He held a hand out, inviting her to join him. She placed her smaller hand in his palm, feeling as if it was symbolic of so much more, and took a step closer. A small line had formed between his brows; he was scowling. Thinking. Deep in analysis.

'I did not expect...' he said, shaking his head again.

He tugged her lightly, pulling her to his body. His hands ran the length of her back gently, carefully.

'Here.' He swallowed, his Adam's apple bobbing visibly as he tried to gain a perspective on this turn of events. He guided her into the shower without breaking his contact with her.

He had one of those enormous ceiling shower heads; warm water doused her the minute she stepped in and she made a little yelp of surprise. Her dark hair was plastered to her face. But once she became accustomed to it the feeling of warmth on her skin was beautiful.

She watched as Nikos took a soft sponge from the shelf and poured shower gel on it. His eyes clung to hers.

'I do not understand,' he said finally, bringing the sponge to her shoulders and soaping her slowly.

The shower gel frothed against her skin. It smelled of lime and vanilla.

'I'm sorry,' Marnie said, then wished she could take the words of contrition back. She bit down on her lower lip. 'Not that I think I did anything wrong,' she hastened to correct. 'Only that I probably should have warned you.'

'Warned me?' A smile flicked at the corners of his lips. 'You think this is something for which I needed *warning*?'

'Well…' She huffed, crossing her arms over her chest. 'I don't know.'

Her eyes dropped to the tiled floor, where the soapy water was fleeing the scene, racing towards the drain.

'Not warning,' he said firmly. 'Just…explanation. How is this possible?'

Her cheeks were glowing; she could feel them. 'Well, it's not that difficult. I've just abstained from having sex. Hardly rocket science.'

His laugh was thick and throaty. Desire flickered in her abdomen, surprising her into blinking her eyes up at him. The air around them seemed to be supercharged with awareness.

He sponged across her décolletage, then lower, slowly, torturously circling one already over-sensitive breast.

'Was it a decision you made? To remain a virgin?'

She was on a precipice. The question wasn't a simple one to answer. If she responded with the truth it would reveal so much more of her heart than she wished to show him! What if she were to tell him that she'd never met a man who'd made her feel remotely tempted in the way he had?

Instinctively she shied away from handing him such a degree of power. 'Yes. I made a little pre-nup with myself,' she breathed with a hint of sarcasm.

He transferred the sponge to her other breast, his attention focussed on the small orbs and the erect nipples that were straining for his touch.

'You wanted to sleep with me back then.'

She shrugged. Her heart was pounding, though. Why hadn't she realised that he would hone in on that? 'Any chance we can *not* talk about this?'

He opened his mouth to say something, but then he nodded, a muscle jerking in his cheek. 'I was surprised,' he said simply. 'You've had boyfriends?'

'Of course I have,' she said, thinking of the handful of men she'd gone on dates with. The men her father had approved of. Suitable men who had left her stone-cold.

'Then how…?'

'I thought we weren't talking about this?' she reminded him quietly.

He nodded once more, his frustration obvious despite his acquiescence. 'It's just so unusual. You are twenty-three years old.'

She nodded, but speech was becoming difficult as he moved the sponge lower, dragging soapy suds over her stomach and lower still, to the space between her legs.

The warm water was heaven against her body. She moaned as he dropped the sponge to the ground with a splash and let his palm rub against her womanhood instead. After wondering briefly if she should be ashamed of the certainty that she wanted him again, she discarded the thought, pressing herself lower, begging him with her body not to remove his hand.

He watched as a fever of desire stole through her body. 'You must have been tempted. From what I recall you had a healthy sexual appetite when we were together.'

She gasped as he teased a finger at her entrance, incapable of responding.

'I had imagined you to have slept with several men by now.'

How those thoughts had tortured him!

'Yes, well…' She groaned, lowering her hips, begging

him for more. 'We're not all as libidinous as you.' She pushed the words out from between clamped teeth.

'*You* are,' he said simply, marvelling at how her body was clamping around him.

He dragged his lips along her jaw, nipping the flesh just beneath her ear before taking an earlobe into his mouth and flicking it between his teeth.

She writhed against the tiles and he jerked in immediate response.

'I would take you again already if I weren't worried about hurting you.'

'You won't hurt me,' she promised throatily. Her eyes were enormous as they lifted to his. 'I want you. *Now.*'

He arched a brow, moving his mouth to her breasts. The soap had long since been washed away and they were warm and moist between his lips. The feeling of his lips on her flesh made her jerk.

'Nik!' she cried out, digging her nails into his shoulder.

The name jarred. *No.* Out of nowhere, it infuriated him. A white-hot rage slammed against him—completely inappropriate but impossible to ignore.

Just her simple use of that name—as though she was slipping back into the past and forgetting that they were no longer a couple. Yes, they were married, but resentment had led to that. Anger, and even hatred. Referring to him as she had done when they were together wasn't something he welcomed.

Nik she'd called him back then. Never Nikos. And her lips had always curved into a sweet smile, as though his name was an invocation of secrets and hopes.

But that had all been a lie. She hadn't really cared for him then; she'd just made him believe she had. She'd played the part perfectly. And he'd fallen for it hook, line and sinker. Well, not again.

She had married him, but only for the sake of her father.

Just as she'd broken up with him because of her father. This was a business deal, plain and simple, and just as in business he needed to keep his focus. Her virginity, while interesting, did not change a thing about their arrangement.

He lifted her against the tiles and wrapped her legs around his waist, driving into her as though his life depended on taking her, on being one with her. It was just sex, but Nikos didn't want anything else from Marnie, anyway. And, no matter how great the sex was, he couldn't forget that.

It was up to him to remember just who he'd married.

She was cold to the core—except in his bed.

CHAPTER FIVE

MARNIE PADDED DOWN the stairs, her eyes straining a little against the brightness of Greece and the whiteness of his home. It was warm, too, though a breeze shifted through the wide corridor, lifting her Donna Karan dress as she reached the ground floor.

The house was quiet, except for a buzzing noise coming from the direction of the kitchen. Curious, she followed the sound, her tummy making a little groan of anticipation.

She'd slept late.

Then again, she'd been up late, too.

Her cheeks flushed as she remembered making love to Nikos in the shower, and then afterwards, when she'd almost drifted off to sleep, she'd felt his mouth teasing her body, drifting over her breasts, down her abdomen, to torment her one last time.

It had been a fantasy. She could almost believe she'd dreamed the whole thing. Except that she felt a little sore and tender in the light of day.

The sight of her husband in the kitchen made her heart skid to a stop. She swallowed, drinking him in hungrily. Awareness flooded her body. He was dressed in a business shirt, the sleeves rolled up to his elbows, exposing those dark, muscled forearms of his. The shirt sat tucked in at the waist, revealing that honed stomach and firm hips. A burst of adrenalin and desire flared through her.

She bit down on her lower lip in an attempt to stall the smile that was threatening to split her mouth apart.

'Morning,' she murmured, her eyes sparkling with re-membered intimacies.

He flicked a gaze to her, then returned his attention to the broadsheet paper that was spread across the bench. 'Coffee?'

Her smile was quick to snap into a small frown. 'Oh… um…yes.'

She wasn't sure he'd heard; he remained perfectly still, his head bent as he read an article. After several long seconds he sipped his own coffee, then placed the mug down and moved to the corner of the kitchen. She'd expected to see a machine, but she saw Nikos had one of those stain-less steel coffee pots. He poured a measure for Marnie and she wrinkled her nose, remembering instantly his predi-lection for coffee so thick it was almost like tar.

'Perhaps I'll have tea instead.'

He shrugged. 'I would be surprised if you find tea-bags. I don't drink the stuff.' He left the coffee cup on the bench beside her, then topped up his own mug. 'Speak to Eléni about your requirements. She will see the house has whatever you need.'

'Eléni?' Marnie murmured, her voice soft in response to his emotional distance.

'My housekeeper,' he reminded her.

'Right.' She nodded, sipping her coffee and pulling a face at the liquid, claggy against her tongue.

Her eyes lifted to the window, and beyond it to the view. The beach was shimmering in the distance, invitingly cool given the warmth of the day.

'I'm happy to go shopping.' A frown pulled at her brows. She wasn't sure she wanted to leave a housekeeper to run the house completely. 'I suppose we should talk about that, actually.'

He gave no indication that he'd heard her. Whatever he was reading was apparently engrossing. Or he was avoiding her like the plague. But that didn't make sense. Not after what they'd shared the night before.

'Nik?' she murmured, moving to stand right beside him.

There it was again. The word that he hated hearing from her mouth. *Nik.* The name that had given him such pleasure in the past was now like an accusing dagger in his gut. A reminder of what they'd been contrasted with what they were now, of the pain of their history and the resentment that had fuelled this union—all contained in that small, soft sound. *Nik.*

Harsh emotions straightened his spine. He pressed his finger into the page, marking his spot, then lifted his eyes to her face. He skimmed her features thoughtfully, careful not to betray the emotions that the simple shortening of his name evoked.

'I think we should stick with Nikos, don't you?'

The rebuff stung. No, it *killed.* A part of herself withered like a cut flower deprived of water.

She narrowed her eyes, ignoring the tears she could feel heavy in her throat. 'Are you sure you wouldn't prefer Mr Kyriazis?'

A muscle jerked in his jaw but he returned his gaze to the paper and read on for a few moments before closing the pages and turning around, propping his butt against the edge of the kitchen bench. His eyes locked with hers.

'What did you want to speak to me about, Mrs Kyriazis?'

She swallowed, all desire to act the part of his wife for real evaporating in the face of his coldness. Confusion was swirling through her, biting at her confidence bit by bit.

'The housekeeper,' she said finally, knowing the only thing worse than looking overeager was looking like an idiot who couldn't finish a thought. 'I can do some of her stuff.'

He arched a brow, silently imploring her to continue.

'Well,' she said, bitterly regretting embarking on this path. 'I did my own shopping at home. Most of my cooking, too. I also took over the gardens.'

'You? Who can't tell wisteria from jasmine?' he prompted sceptically.

She squared her shoulders. 'That was a long time ago. I love flowers now. Roses especially.'

She was babbling. What was that pervasive feeling of grief? And how could she stem its tide?

'Do you grow roses here? I suppose not. They're more of an English thing, aren't they? But, anyway, you said you have gardeners. In England I...' She tapered off at his complete lack of responsiveness.

'Eléni has been my housekeeper for a long time,' he said finally, his tone as far from encouraging as it was possible to get. 'I am not willing to offend her. She will not want to share her responsibilities.'

Marnie stared at him with rich disbelief. 'Even with your *wife*?'

His smile was not softened by anything like happiness or pleasure. 'My wife has other responsibilities.'

Marnie reached for her coffee. Thick and gloopy or not, it still had the ability to put some fire in her blood. 'What's got into you?' she asked when she'd drunk almost the whole cup. 'You're treating me like...like...'

He waited for her to continue, but when she didn't speak, letting her sentence trail off into nothingness, he prompted, 'Like what?'

He was impatient now. She felt like a recalcitrant child.

'Like you hate me.'

His nostrils flared as he expelled an angry breath. 'Your

words, *agape*, not mine.' He pushed up off the bench. 'I'll be home for dinner.'

'Where are you going?' She stared at him incredulously.

He laughed. 'Well, Marnie, I have to go to *work*. You see, our so-called marriage is really a business deal. You've upheld your end of the bargain spectacularly well so far— even bringing your virginity to the table. Now it is my turn. My assistant's number is on the fridge, should you need me.'

He walked out of the kitchen without so much as a kiss on the cheek.

She stared at his retreating back, gaping like a fish dragged mercilessly from the water. Hurt flashed inside her, but anger was there, too. How could he be so unkind? They were married, and only hours earlier had been as close as two people could be. That had moved things around for her; it had changed the tone of her heart. She wasn't the same woman she'd been the day before, or the week before, or when they'd made this hateful deal.

But for Nikos apparently nothing had changed. *Nothing.*

And he hadn't even told her to call *him* if she needed anything! She was so far down the pecking order that she was supposed to go through his assistant if she needed her own husband for anything.

Well! She'd show him!

She ground her teeth together and wandered over to the newspaper, simply for something to do. The article he'd been reading was an incredibly dry piece on an Italian bank that was restructuring its sub-prime loans.

She flicked out of the finance section and went to international news. Though she generally liked to keep abreast of world events, she looked at the words that morning without comprehension. The black-and-white letters swam like little bugs in her eyes until she gave up in frustration and slammed the paper shut.

She sipped the coffee again, before remembering how disgusting she found it, and then glided across the kitchen floor, pulling the fridge open. The platters from the night before were there; they'd been put back on their shelves. The flavours were reminiscent of childhood family holidays, when the four of them had travelled by yacht around the Med, stopping off at whichever island had taken their fancy, enjoying the local delicacies.

Libby had loved squid. She'd eaten charcoaled tentacles by the dozen. Whereas Marnie had been one for olives, cheese, bread and *dolmades*. Libby had joked about Marnie's metabolism in a way she'd been too young to understand, though now she knew that she'd been unfairly blessed with the ability to eat what she wanted and not see it in her figure.

It was the one small genetic blessing Marnie had in her favour. The rest had gone to Libby. The shimmering blonde hair that had waved down her back, the enormous bright blue eyes, a curving smile that had seemed to dance like the wind on her face, flicking and freshening with each emotion she felt. And Libby had almost always been happy.

Marnie padded across the tiled floor, drawn to the glass doors that framed the view of the ocean. It sparkled in the distance, and she saw with a little sound of pleasure that there was an infinity pool in the foreground. She toyed with the door handle until it clicked open and then slid the glass aside, stepping out onto the paved terrace as though the breeze had dragged her.

She breathed deeply. Salt and pollution were a heady mix for a girl who'd spent much of her time in the English countryside. She grinned, trying to put her situation with Nikos temporarily out of her mind. An almost childlike curiosity was settling around her, and she slipped across the terrace and stood on the edge of pool. The water was turquoise.

Her toe, almost of its own volition, skimmed the surface before diving beneath, taking her foot with it.

Perfection.

Uncaring that her expensive linen dress might get crumpled or wet, and for once not thinking about photographers or what people might think, safe in the knowledge that she was completely alone, Marnie lifted the dress over her head and left it in a roughly folded heap on the tiles.

In only her bra and underpants she slid into the water, making a little moan of delight as it lapped up to her neck. As a child she'd gone swimming often.

She ducked her head underwater, beyond caring that her artfully applied make-up would smudge, and stroked confidently to the far end of the pool. She propped her chin on the edge, studying the bright blue sky, turquoise ocean and faraway buildings for a moment before duck-diving underwater once more and returning to the house side.

It felt good to swim, and she lost count of how many laps she completed. Eventually, though, as she drew to the edge of the pool, her arms a little wobbly, she paused to gain breath.

'You are fast.'

A woman's accented voice reached her and Marnie started a little, her heart racing at the intrusion.

Not knowing exactly what to expect, she spun in the water until her eyes pinned the source of the voice.

A woman was on the terrace, a mop in one hand, a smile on her lined face. She had long hair, going by the voluminous messy bun that was piled on top of her hair, and it was a grey like lead. She wore a dark blue dress that fell to the knees and sensible sandals.

The housekeeper. What had Nikos said her name was? She wished now she'd paid better attention, rather than focussing her mental skills on just what the hell had happened in the hours since they'd made love.

'You swim like a dolphin, no?' the housekeeper said, and when her smile widened, Marnie saw that she was missing a tooth.

'Thank you,' she said, inwardly wincing at how uptight she sounded. She tried to loosen the effect with a smile of her own. 'I'm Marnie.'

'You Mrs Kyriazis.' The housekeeper nodded. 'I know, I know.'

She was tall and wiry and she moved fast, propping the mop against the side of the house before lifting the lid of a cane basket. 'I always keep towels in here. Mr Kyriazis likes his swim after work.'

Dangerous images of Nikos—bare-chested, water trickling over his muscled chest and honed arms—made her insides squeeze with remembered desire. 'Does he?'

'So the towels always are fresh. I can get you one.'

True to her word, she lifted one from the box and placed it on the edge of the pool, beside Marnie's dress. Her hand ran to the item of clothing, lifting it as if on autopilot and draping it over a chair instead.

Marnie was a little shamefaced at the uncharacteristic way she'd discarded it.

'I'm sorry,' she said, her tone stiff. 'Nikos didn't mention your name,' she fibbed.

'I'm Mrs Adona.' She grinned. 'You can call me Eléni, though, like Mr Kyriazis does.'

'Eléni.' Marnie nodded crisply. *That was it.* Curious, she tilted her head to one side, watching as the older woman returned to fetch the mop. 'It's nice to meet you.'

Eléni cackled quietly in response.

'That's funny?' Marnie prompted with a small smile on her face.

Later, she would be mortified to realise that she had big black circles of smudged mascara beneath each eye.

'Oh, it is nice for me to meet you, I was thinking. Nice for him to settle down. In my day men didn't work as hard as him. They had one woman and a simple job. You'll be good for him,' Eléni said, with an optimism that Marnie was loath to dispel.

So she nodded. 'Perhaps.'

Something occurred to her and, spontaneously, she called the woman nearer to the pool.

'Eléni? Nikos is worried that I'll step on your toes if I do the odd bit of grocery shopping or cooking.'

She watched the other woman carefully for any sign of mortification or offence, and instead saw a broad grin.

Spurred on, she continued, 'The thing is, I quite like to cook. And I don't have a lot to do here yet, and shopping kills time. So…well…I hope you won't be upset if you see that happening?'

'Upset?'

Her laugh was contagious and alarming in equal measure. Loud—so loud it seemed almost amplified—it pealed across the courtyard and out towards the sea. Marnie found herself chuckling in response.

Eléni said something in her own language, then rubbed her angled chin as if searching for the words in English. 'I don't know he can like a woman who cooks.'

The sentence was a little disjointed, and the accent was thick, but the meaning came to Marnie loud and clear.

Nikos didn't bring women who cooked to his home.

They had other talents.

And wasn't that just an unpalatable thought?

Well, Marnie would show him.

By the time he returned that night Marnie and Eléni had moved a table onto the tiled terrace and Eléni had set it beautifully. A crisp white cloth fell to the floor, and in its centre she'd placed orange blossoms and red geraniums to create an artful and fragrant arrangement of blooms.

Marnie was just pulling the scallops Mornay from the grill when he arrived. It was difficult to say who was more surprised. Nikos, by the sight of his wife in a black-and-white apron, kitchen glove on one hand, feet bare but for the red toenail polish that was strangely seductive, or Marnie, who took one look at her husband and felt such a surge of emotions that she had to prop her hip on the bench behind her for support.

He placed a black leather bag on the kitchen floor, then crossed his arms. 'I thought we discussed this,' he said finally.

So much for new beginnings.

'*You* discussed it, as I remember.' Her smile was overly saccharine. 'I listened while you told me that I shouldn't get comfortable in your home.'

Her acerbic remark had caught him unawares—that much was obvious.

Choosing not to tackle the bigger issue of her statement, he said thickly, 'I told you—I don't want you upsetting Eléni .'

'Yes, yes...' She moved to the fridge and pulled a bottle of ice-cold champagne from the door. She placed it in his hand and paused right in front of him. 'You also told me that I should save my energy for other wifely duties.'

He had. And he'd enjoyed, in some small part, seeing the way he'd shocked her. But having her say the words back to him switched everything around. A hint of shame whispered across his features.

'Eléni's very happy that you've married someone who enjoys cooking,' she said, with an exaggerated batting of her long, silky lashes. 'I think she finds me surprisingly traditional compared to your usual...*companions*.'

'You've spoken to her?' he said unnecessarily.

'Yes. So you don't need to worry that I've sent her off to cry into her pillows.'

He curled his fingers around the neck of the bottle and unfurled the foiled top, his eyes lingering on his wife's face. Her honey-brown hair was plaited and little tendrils had escaped, curling around her eyes. Her make-up was impeccable, and beneath the apron he could see that she was wearing a simple dress that he was growing impatient to remove.

'You have a smudge on your cheek,' he lied, lifting his thumb to his mouth to wet it before wiping it across her skin. He was rewarded with the sight of her eyes fluttering closed and her full lips parting as she exhaled softly. The same knot of desire that had sat in his gut all day was inside her, too, then.

'I've been busy,' she said softly, her eyes bouncing open and clashing with his. As if consciously slicing through the web that was thick around them, she stepped backwards. 'You open that—thank you.'

A grudging smile lifted half his mouth. 'Yes, Mrs Kyriazis.'

She turned away before he could see the way the name brought an answering smile to her own features.

He popped the top off the bottle, placed the cork on the bench. He reached for two glasses at the same time she did. Their hands connected and she stepped aside quickly. 'You do it. I'll get our starter.'

'Starter?' he murmured, watching as a pink like the sunset dusted her cheekbones.

'Uh-huh. I told you—I like to cook.'

That was new. 'Since when?'

She began to place the scallops in their fan-like shells on a plate, forming a spiral of sorts. 'Some time after we broke up—' she skidded over the words a little awkwardly

'—I discovered it as a hobby. It turns out I love cooking. I've always loved food.'

She reached for a spoon and ran it around the edge of a shell, coating it in the Mornay sauce. She lifted it to his lips and he widened his mouth to taste the sauce. It was as delicious as it smelled.

'Apparently you excel at it.'

'Thank you.' The compliment was a gift. A beautiful gift to cherish in the midst of the turbulent ocean they were stranded in. She lifted the plate and smiled. 'Shall we?'

He turned, two champagne flute stems trapped between the fingers of one hand, the bottle in his other. He began to retreat from the kitchen, but Marnie stalled him.

'Not the dining room,' she said over her shoulder, weaving through the kitchen towards the patio. It was then that Nikos saw that against the backdrop of the setting sun, and the evening sky that sparkled with tiny little diamonds of stardust, a table glowed with candlelight.

Emotions, warm and fierce, surged in his chest. '*You* did this?'

'Eléni helped,' she said honestly, nudging the door with her shoulder.

The night was blissfully warm. She placed the scallops on the table and then stretched behind her back for the ties of the apron.

'Allow me,' he said throatily, settling the drinks onto the table and reaching for her. His fingers worked deftly at the strings but, once they were untied, he kept his hands on her hips. He spun her in the circle of his arms so that he could stare down at her face. In the softness of dusk she was breathtakingly beautiful. But the fragility he sensed in her terrified him.

He wasn't prepared for Marnie's vulnerability. He had no protection against it.

He dropped his hands to his sides and moved to a chair instead. He pulled it from the table, waiting for her to settle herself in the seat. She pushed the apron over her head, not minding that it roughened her hair. She draped it over the timber back of the chair, keeping her eyes on the spectacular view as she sat down.

He glided the chair inwards a little way, his hands resting on her bare shoulders for a moment before he moved to the other side of the table.

At another time, or for another pair, the moment would have been singing with romance. But Marnie knew they didn't qualify for that. And yet the setting was so magical that for a moment she let herself forget the tension and the blackmail, the resentments and regrets.

'Do you remember when we had that picnic in Brighton?'

His eyes skimmed her face, tracing the features he'd stared at that night. It had been only a few weeks before he'd told her he wanted to marry her one day—before she'd told him that would never happen.

'Yes.' He pressed back in his chair. The past was a sharp course he didn't particularly like to contemplate. 'I remember.'

'The sun was a little like this,' she said, obviously not sensing his tone, or perhaps willfully ignoring it.

She watched the glow of the golden orb as its own weight seemed to catch up with it, making it impossible for day to remain any longer. As the sun dipped gratefully towards the sea the sky seemed to serenade it, whispering peach and purple against its outline.

'This is my favourite thing to watch,' she said softly, a self-conscious smile ghosting across her face as she returned her attention to the table.

'Why?'

She lifted a scallop and placed it on her plate, indicating that he should do likewise. But he was fully focussed on his bride.

'I guess I find it somehow reassuring,' she said with a small shrug of her slender shoulders. 'That no matter what happens in a day there'll always be this.'

He arched a brow, finding the sentiment both beautiful and depressing. 'I am more for mornings,' he said after a moment.

'I remember.' She grinned, trying hard to inject their evening with the normality she'd longed for that morning. 'You wake before the sun.'

'I do not need a lot of sleep.'

'Apparently.'

Her cheeks flushed pink as she remembered the previous night—the way he had commanded her body's full attention even when she had been exhausted. And she'd responded to his invitations willingly, rousing herself to join with him, needing him even from behind the veil of exhaustion.

He ate a scallop, though he wasn't particularly hungry. It was divine. A perfect combination of sweetness and salt. He didn't say anything, though, so Marnie continued to wonder if he'd enjoyed it or was simply being polite when he reached for another.

'How was your day?' she asked, after a moment of prickly silence had passed.

He regarded her for a long moment. 'I spoke with your father, if that is your concern.'

Her face slashed with hurt before she concealed it expertly. 'It wasn't,' she responded, shrugging as though he *hadn't* scratched her with the sharp blade of recrimination. 'I was simply making conversation.'

His eyes glowed with the strength of his feelings. Marnie pressed back in her chair, her own appetite waning. She

thought of the fish she was baking in a salt crust. What a
waste it would be if they couldn't even make it through a
few scallops without breaking into war.

'Let us not pretend, Marnie, when there is no one here
to benefit from the performance.'

CHAPTER SIX

She placed her fork down carefully beside the plate, using the distraction to rally her rioting emotions. His mood and manner were on a knife's edge. She felt the shift in him and wanted to protest. She wanted to address it. But the implacable set of his features thwarted any thought of that.

'I'm not pretending,' she said instead, with a direct stare that cost her a great deal of effort.

'Of course you are.' He was bored now, or at least he seemed it.

'Really? Why? Because I asked about your day?'

His eyes narrowed. 'Because you act as though your primary concern in this marriage is not your father.'

Denying that assertion wasn't an option—at least it wasn't if she wanted to protect herself from seeming motivated by other more personal feelings. What would he say if she told him more than money had motivated her into marrying him? Would he run a mile? Or use her confused feelings to keep her exactly where he had her?

'Well, Nikos,' she said, impressed that she sounded almost condescending, 'given that you used my father's debts to blackmail me into this, are you really so surprised?'

'I made no claim of surprise,' he corrected. 'I intended to point out the futility of your charade.'

'Wow.' She blinked and lifted her champagne, drinking

several large gulps despite the pain of the bubbles erupting against her insides. 'That's spectacularly rude,' she said when she'd settled the glass back on the table.

'Perhaps.' He shrugged insouciantly. 'In any event, your father was both grateful and, I believe, resentful of my offer to help.'

She was startled, her enormous eyes flying to his face. 'You're not saying he turned you down?'

'He has agreed to take the bare minimum from me to stave off foreclosure. That will buy him another month at the most.' A frown crossed his features. 'He is a stubborn man.'

'Remind you of anyone?' she snapped tartly, biting into another scallop.

'I would not be so foolish as to turn away a lifeline if I were in his situation.'

'He's very proud,' she said silkily, and though she'd meant it to be a subtle insult to Nikos it was ridiculous. She'd realised as soon as she'd uttered the words. For there was no man on earth with more pride than Nikos. She'd damaged it six years earlier and he'd moved heaven and earth to make her pay now.

'To a fault.'

'Thank you for speaking to him,' she said quietly.

She meant it. Were it not for Nikos, her father would have no hope. At least he knew now that there was an option. An alternative to bleak bankruptcy and failure.

'It was our deal, remember?'

The deal. The damned deal! She wanted to tear her hair out! But why? One day after their wedding, did she *really* think anything would have shifted? Just because they'd slept together, and her body had begun to vibrate at a frequency that only he could answer, it didn't mean that it was the same for him.

'Nonetheless, you didn't have to do this. Any of it. You

could have left him to suffer and watched from the side-lines.'

He braced his elbows on the table, his eyes pinning her to the chair as though his fingers were curled around her shoulders. 'Where would the fun be in that?'

The air crackled and hummed with the intensity of his statement.

'You find this *fun*?'

His smile was pure sensual seduction. Like warmed chocolate being dripped over her flesh.

'Last night was certainly pleasurable.'

Memories seared her soul. She shifted a little in the chair as her insides slicked with pleasurable anticipation. 'I'm glad you think so,' she murmured, her heart racing like a butterfly trapped against a window.

His smile was pure arrogance. It said that he knew she thought so, too. 'You disagree?'

Damn it. The wedge between a rock and hard place was a little constricting. She dropped her gaze, unable and un-willing to duel with him in a battle she'd never win.

But Nikos wasn't going to let it go. 'You seemed to enjoy yourself...' he pushed, one hand flicking lazily across the tablecloth, trapping her fingers beneath his. He turned her palm skywards and began to trace an in-visible circle across the soft pad of her hand.

'Now who's acting?' Her question was breathy, infused with the hot air in her lungs.

'When it comes to my desire for you there is no neces-sity to lie.'

'Thank heavens for small mercies.' The statement was lacking sass; it fell flat. She cleared her throat and pulled her hand away. 'How much money?'

The change in conversation, and the removal of her hand, confused him momentarily. But not for long. Nikos hadn't built an empire from scratch by being slow on the uptake.

'Why does it matter? Do you want to make sure you haven't overpaid your end of our bargain?'

She made a sound of surprise and shook her head.

'You did offer your virginity. Perhaps you feel anything less than a hundred mill isn't quite fair on you.'

'How *dare* you?' Her voice quivered with the force of her hurt. 'How dare you equate what we did with an amount of money?'

He had gone too far. He realised that, but it was out of Nikos's character to apologise. Instead he came back to the original question, speaking as though he *hadn't* just virtually equated their marriage with prostitution.

'I have helped him enough for now,' he said, his words soft to placate the rage he'd breathed into her. 'He will not go broke, Marnie. I will not allow that to happen.'

She pulled her lower lip between her teeth, her feelings jumping awkwardly from one extreme to the other. Hurt was making her body sag, and her throat was thick with tears that she damned well would *not* let fall. But there was relief and gratitude, too. Because she *did* trust Nikos. Despite all this, all that he'd done, she believed that he would keep her father from destitution.

He lifted another scallop and ate it, then another, and Marnie watched, a frown unconsciously etched across her face.

'Are you going to have any more?' he prompted, reaching for the second-last.

She shook her head. 'I'm fine, thanks.'

He placed his fork down and stared at her. 'Your father has asked us to return to England for his birthday.'

Marnie nodded thoughtfully. 'He doesn't like to do much, but Mum generally twists his arm into a small party.'

His expression was guarded. 'Would you like to travel home again so soon?'

Home.

The word was one syllable that throbbed with an enormous weight of meaning. She reached for the last scallop, despite having just given up her claim to it. She needed to distract herself and to hide her face as she unpacked the impact that single word was having.

Home.

Other than here.

Home.

Not here. Not in *his* home.

She blinked and shook her head a tiny bit, pushing the thoughts away. 'I'd like to see them,' she said cautiously. 'But it *is* soon. I didn't really imagine that we'd go to England again yet.'

Her family complicated matters. What hope did Nikos and she have of forming any kind of relationship with her parents and his antipathy towards them in the foreground?

'You want to refuse?'

She toyed with her ring, turning it round her finger. 'I didn't say that.'

'No. You didn't say anything,' he drawled, the words lightly teasing.

But Marnie was not in the mood to be teased.

'God, Nikos, you're impossible.'

He laughed throatily, the sound doing something strange to her fractured nerves.

'I am honestly asking what you would like. It occurred to me that I would have more success persuading your father to be reasonable if we were to meet in person.'

The tears he'd brought to the surface were closer now, and she had to dig her nails into her palms to stop from weakening and letting her eyes become moist.

Out of habit, she hardened her expression, creating an

air of nonchalance when she tilted her face to his. 'You'd do that?'

His eyes glittered in his handsome face. 'You'd be content if I didn't?'

Damn it. She was being careless. Slowly she shook her head from side to side, her eyes not quite meeting his. 'You told me you'd sort it out. It's the only reason I married you, remember?'

'Good. Honesty is so much better than role-play.'

She cleared her throat and focussed her gaze on the view. What she'd just said hadn't been honesty, but she let it slide. 'Fine. We'll go back for a weekend. In a month.'

And in the back of her mind she really did hope that their difficulties might have been resolved by then. There had been a time when they were so comfortable together. Was it so unlikely to believe they might return to that footing?

She looked at the man opposite, her heart turning over in her chest.

So familiar.

So foreign.

She knew him intimately, and yet she didn't.

He was a stranger, and yet her husband.

The dichotomies kept flowing through her mind, thick and fast.

'You are staring, Mrs Kyriazis, in a way that makes me want to peel that dress from your body and claim you here and now.'

She started, her pulse shearing her skin. 'I was just thinking…' Her voice was thick with the desire he could so easily evoke. 'So much has happened in six years. You're my husband, and at one time I would have said I knew you better than anyone. But I don't know you at all now.'

'You know me,' he responded, standing up swiftly and reaching for her plate.

She watched as he cleared the table, her mind overflowing with questions.

'When we were together, you only had aspirations in finance. How did you do all this so fast?'

He sent her a look of impatience. 'When someone tells you that you will never amount to anything, that you are not worth a damn, it *is* rather motivating.'

Her father's words mortified her. 'He shouldn't have said that.'

'No.' His eyes glittered. 'But that is what you people are like. Do you *really* believe that the blood in your veins is of more value than mine simply because you can trace your lineage back thousands of years and I am not able to do so?'

'Don't do that.' She followed him into the kitchen. 'Don't tar me with the same brush.' A frown drew her brows together. 'I don't really understand why my dad spoke like that to you. He's not—'

'Of course he is,' Nikos interrupted. He tamped down on his temper with effort, stacking the plates neatly into the dishwasher.

He worked with a finesse that made her wonder if he did this simple domestic act often. Though incongruous, it made sense. Nikos hadn't been born with a silver spoon in his mouth. He'd grown up poor. He'd presumably shouldered his fair share of domestic duties for most of his life.

'Whatever you're about to say, make no mistake. He *is*.'

'Anyway…' She made an effort to salvage the situation. 'I understand why you might have felt you had to prove something. But *how* did you do this?'

His eyes skimmed her face. 'In the same way I won a scholarship to Eton and then Cambridge. I worked a thousand times harder than anyone else. I always have. I don't sleep much, *agape*, because I work.'

Admiration soared through her. 'I think you've done something very impressive,' she said quietly.

He propped himself against a bench. 'Your turn. Why did *you* do all this?' He gestured around the kitchen.

Because I missed you. Because I couldn't stop thinking about you.

'It's our honeymoon, isn't it?'

His lips lifted in a half-smile. 'If you say so.'

The rejection hurt, but she didn't show it. 'Why don't you sit down? I'll get the main course.'

He crossed the kitchen so that he stood right in front of her, without touching. Goose bumps littered her exposed flesh.

'I have a better idea.'

She lifted her eyes to his face slowly. Breathing was suddenly difficult. He overwhelmed every single sense in her body. 'Oh?'

'Let's have a break between courses.' His smile was tight. 'I do not usually eat so early.'

'Oh…'

He'd upset her. He squashed the urge to apologise. 'It is a…ritual I have. I swim as soon as I return from the office. I find it rids me of the day.' He reached down and linked his fingers. 'Join me.'

A command or a question?

An order or an invitation?

Whatever the case, she found herself nodding. 'Okay. I'll just go and get changed.'

His laugh was throaty. 'Why?'

Her eyes were wide. She watched as he began slowly to unbutton his shirt until the sides were separated. He pushed it off his arms, then stepped out of his trousers. In just his boxers, he reached over and lifted her hand to his lips.

His kiss breathed butterflies into her veins. She stifled a moan and then pulled at her hand. It was a necessary tool. She felt around for her zip, and when she couldn't immediately catch it he reached behind her and loosened it, sliding it slowly, seductively, teasingly down her spine.

She shivered as his fingers lingered, taunting the flesh at the small of her back. She lifted her gaze to his face again, searching for something there. Kindness? Affection? She saw only lust. Pure and simple.

It was better than nothing.

With a small exhalation she stepped backwards. 'I'll just need a minute.' She took another step backwards to underscore her resolve. 'I'll meet you in there.'

He shrugged indolently and strode across the tiles with that almost feral power that seemed to emanate from his frame. She watched him go, greedily waiting to see him dive into the water. His muscles rippled as he speared through the air then beneath its surface. She held her breath unconsciously until he stood at the other end. His dark hair was slicked to his head like an animal's pelt.

She moved quickly up the stairs and into their bedroom. The sight of her face that had confronted her after swimming earlier that day was hauntingly close to the surface. She didn't want to turn into a panda again. She lathered her hands with soap and washed at her face until every hint of make-up was removed, then changed into a swimsuit with a low-cut vee at the front and delicate beading in the fabric. It was elegant and inviting.

He was swimming laps when she emerged, his strong body pulling powerfully through the water, each bronzed arm worthy of its own sculpture. He was naked. His boxers had been discarded and she could see his whole body as he cut through the water.

She swallowed huskily, her eyes tracing his progress from where she stood at the edge of the pool. A warm breeze drifted past, lifting her hair. She tucked it behind her ears and approached the edge. He turned underwater, his stroke not breaking the surface.

With a smile, she dived in, pulling up beside him. Underwater, their faces were illuminated by the green lights embedded in the side of the pool. He turned to her. Their eyes locked and Marnie almost lost her rhythm, so fierce was the tumble of awareness that accosted her body.

But she quickly regained her focus, racing him to the end and touching the rounded edge of the pool just as he did. She laughed when they both lifted onto their feet, the thrill of adrenalin and the rush of endorphins pumping through her body.

He stared at her with a sense of confusion.

Her laugh.

That beautiful laugh.

It was as if she'd burst through the cracks in his memory, slowly infiltrating him with what she'd once meant to him.

It wasn't only the musical sound, it was her face. Wiped of make-up, radiating happiness, with a little bit of honey in her complexion from the day she'd spent outdoors.

He swallowed and turned to the view, his face unyielding in profile.

'I haven't swum like this in years,' she confided easily, blissfully unaware of the hurricane of feelings that was besieging him.

His smile lacked warmth. He pinned her with eyes that she couldn't read. A sense of loss wiped the smile from her own features and she spun away, kicking to the opposite side of the pool and propping herself against it. The coping was still warm from the day's heat, despite the lateness of the hour and the coldness of his look.

The sense that her husband—the man she'd married and had once loved—despised her, made her heart hurt in her chest. She turned slowly to see him walking through the water towards her, his gaze pinned to hers.

He was going to kiss her. The fine pulse at the base of her throat was hammering wildly in expectation, and yet every sensible thread of her mind was telling her to step backwards and talk to him.

What did it mean that she had such a small understanding of everything that made him tick except his desire for her?

'Nikos,' she said softly, her eyes silently imploring him to help her make sense of it all.

He caught her hips underwater, pulling her the final distance to meet him. Their bodies melded as one. She drew her lip between her teeth, ignoring the warning voice in her mind as she wrapped her arms around his neck. Her fingers teased the wet hair at his nape.

'I know.'

Her breath hitched in her throat. She wasn't alone. This maelstrom of need after six long years was as unsettling for him as it was her.

Good.

For now that would have to be enough.

His kiss was a claim. It was a seal of their union. She kissed him back fiercely, her tongue clashing with his, her body wrapping around his beneath the water. The feeling of his arousal between her legs, straining at the fabric of her swimsuit, with the warmth of the pool water surrounding them was almost too much to bear.

Impatience crested inside her, bubbling out of control.

She made a sound into his mouth as she pushed back a little, her fingers toying with the straps of her swimsuit. They were saturated, and stuck to her body like a second skin; it didn't help that her hands were unsteady.

He had no such difficulty.

With total confidence he slid the straps down her arms,

revealing her breasts. The dusk light bathed her, spreading gold and peach over her flesh. He continued to push the fabric away, and Marnie lifted her legs to make it easier.

Naked in the water with him, she had a blinding sense that she might actually die if they didn't make love. If something were to happen to change his mind she wasn't sure she could recover. Her desperation for him would have terrified her if she'd had any mental space left with which to process it.

He pulled her back towards him, settling her legs around his waist. His eyes showed strain as he paused, his hard cock nestled between her legs without yet invading her womanhood.

'You have not been sore today?'

She shook her head.

'You must tell me...'

Groaning, she repositioned herself, startling him by thrusting down on his length and taking him deep inside her core. Relief spread through her body, weakening and strengthening her in yet another contradictory sensation. He held her hips, his fingers digging into her soft flesh, his lips seeking hers. His tongue was harsh in her mouth, echoing the movements of his body as he made her completely his.

Her orgasm burst over her swiftly; there was no time to prepare.

The entire day had been a kind of torturous foreplay for Marnie. Memories of their night together had tormented her, driving her body to fever pitch, so that the tiniest things—such as the feeling of the apron as she'd wrapped it around her over-sensitised nipples—had almost driven her over the edge.

Nikos watched as she crested the wave, her face a thousand little nerve endings vibrating with pleasure. The answering swelling in his heart was not something he wished to acknowledge.

Telling himself it was simply relief that they'd found themselves to be sexually compatible, he pushed deeper into her, drifting his fingers lower to cup the neat softness of her buttocks. He dragged his lips down her throat, flicking his tongue against the pulse-point that was frantically trying to move blood through her body, then lower still to her breasts. They were lapped by the water, and he had to lift her a little to take one into his mouth. The second he did she cried out, tilting her wet head back into the water so that her hair, no longer braided, fell like a dark curtain.

He moved one hand to tangle in its lengths, holding her head there while he plundered her core in an insatiable rhythm.

His own control was slipping. Her muscles, so moist and tight, were squeezing him as her pleasure spiralled, and when he felt her tremble and knew she was about to crest the wave again he went with her, holding her close, mirroring her movements until they were both panting, drenched in sweat and pool water, satisfaction emanating from every pore.

Their coming together had been as intense as it had essential. But it was just a prelude to the slow exploration he had been distracted by thinking of all day. To the myriad ways he wanted to torment and delight her.

Satiated, Marnie slowly relaxed, her body reassuring her that nothing bad could eventuate when such uncontainable desire abounded.

It was only then that she remembered the fish in the oven. It would be burned to a crisp.

Well, if that was the only casualty of this desire then she could live with it.

In the small hours of the morning, their naked limbs tangled with crisp white sheets, bodies sheened in post-coital perspiration and satisfaction, sleep fogging around the edges of their tableau, Marnie shifted a little, tilting her head to observe her husband.

His eyes were shut, his breathing heavy.

'How can you call this a pretence?' she whispered—to herself more than anything.

Without opening his eyes, he said thickly, 'This is just great sex, Marnie. Do not confuse it with anything more substantive or you will be hurt.'

He rolled over, his broad, muscled back turned to her, his heart apparently closed.

CHAPTER SEVEN

A FORTNIGHT HAD passed and his words were still sharp in her brain, like shards of glass that made her weep blood whenever she ran the fingertip of her mind over them.

'This is just great sex... Do not confuse it with anything more substantive...'

Her coffee-coloured eyes were flecked with gold as they drifted over the view from the window. For her office she'd chosen a room far away from the pool, their bedroom and the kitchen—that was to say far from any of the rooms that distracted her with what Nikos and she had shared there.

It was a small room, but she didn't need a lot of space, and it afforded an outlook of the city, rather than the ocean. In the distance she could see the Acropolis, bathed in early-evening light, and the buildings of the city sprawled almost like a child's model.

Though she took solace and inspiration from the outlook, this was not why she'd chosen this particular spot from which to work. From her seat she could see the curve of Nikos's driveway. The second his car thrummed through the gates she knew. And then she had the maximum time to prepare herself for his arrival, to gather the facade she had perfected around her slender shoulders. A facade that was essential when faced with her husband.

They shared meals and polite conversation. They were

unstintingly civil. But there was a torrent of emotions swirling hatefully beneath all their appropriate conversations. Only when they came together at night did she find an outlet for her rampant emotions. Sex. Passionate, all-consuming sex that explained everything. She was addicted to him. To his body and to the way he made her feel.

Marnie clicked out of her spreadsheet, her mind half-absorbed with the call-list she had for the following day. How grateful she was to have her work! Were it not for the distraction of the behind-the-scenes fundraising she did for the Future Trust she might have exploded already in a scene reminiscent of Vesuvius.

She flicked a glance to the clock above the door. He was late, and nerves that had been stretched tight for two days—since he'd told her about this event—were at breaking point.

For the first time since marrying they were going *out*.

Strange how she hadn't even realised that she'd become a virtual recluse, spending her time almost exclusively within the confines of his home except for brief trips to the markets with Eléni.

Now it was time to meet the world. She was Mrs Kyriazis—billionaire's wife.

What a joke.

Their marriage was little more than revenge and sex, and yet tonight she would play the part of doting newly-wed to perfection. If only to show him how little she cared.

She heard his car and rose quickly from her desk. It wasn't that she had intended to be secretive about her work, but Nikos never came into her office. As if that conversation on her first afternoon in Greece had flagged something in his mind and he had subsequently delineated her office as her own space. For all he knew she might be running some kind of international drug ring, she thought with a small smile as she pulled the door shut behind her.

Marnie rarely wore heels, but for the kind of evening Nikos had foreshadowed she knew they'd be a requirement. They did bolster her height nicely, and she felt the picture of elegance when she walked gracefully down the stairs.

She'd spent a long time styling her hair, and her make-up was a masterpiece. Anne Kenington might not have played Cubby House with her children, nor had she read them the books that a nanny had had more time for, but she had insisted both her daughters were drilled in the skills necessary to present themselves as Ladies.

When Marnie emerged into the foyer at the same moment that Nikos entered the house she waited with a small smile on her red lips for him to see her. Pleasant anticipation swirled through her as she waited for the light of attraction to bounce between them.

The second his eyes lifted to her she felt a bolt of something. Not desire. Not happiness. Something else. Something far darker.

His eyes undertook a slow and thorough inspection, but his expression showed only shock. Marnie held her breath as he stared at her, waiting, aching, needing. Wanting him to say something to explain the reaction.

'You look...' He wiped a hand across his eyes and shook his head.

'Yes?' She braved a smile, though her heart was plummeting to the floor.

'Nothing. It doesn't matter.'

He dropped his keys onto the side table and turned away. Only the ragged movement of his chest showed that he was still struggling with a dark tangle of emotions.

'I will be ready as soon as I can. Why do you not have a drink while you wait?'

A frown marred her features for the briefest of moments before she remembered. She didn't *do* that! She didn't betray how easily he could upset her.

'Fine,' she agreed, her smile ice-cold, her pulse hammering. 'Don't be long. You said it starts at eight.'

He didn't acknowledge her rejoinder. Marnie watched with consternation as he took the stairs two at a time, then she turned away and wove her way to the kitchen.

It was another stunning evening. The sun was almost completely out of sight, leaving inky streaks in the sky and a sprinkling of sparkling lights that heralded night's arrival. She flicked the kettle on to brew tea and then thought better of it. She had a feeling something stronger was called for.

She poured a glass of champagne and held it in both hands as she moved to the terrace. The pool was beautiful. The surface, undisturbed by their usual evening activity, had a stillness to it, and it reflected not only the evening sky and the glow of his house but Marnie's figure, too.

She stared down at the watery image of herself, allowing her earlier frown to tug her lips downwards now that she was alone. Why did he disapprove? Though she hated this sort of mix-and-mingle affair, she'd been to enough of them to know the drill. Her dress was the latest word in couture, her shoes were perfect—everything about her was just what people would expect the wife of Nikos Kyriazis to be.

She crouched down, careful to keep the hem of her dress out of the water, and ran her manicured fingertips through its surface, slashing her image so that only swirls of colour remained. Satisfied, she stood and turned towards the house, startled when she saw Nikos just inside the door.

He'd showered and changed into a formal tuxedo, and his dark hair was slicked back from his brow, showing the hauteur of his handsome features, the strength of his bone structure and the determination of his jaw.

A kaleidoscope of butterflies was swirling through her insides, filling her veins with flutters of anticipation. As she stepped closer a hint of his fragrance—that unmistakably masculine scent of spice and citrus—carried to her on the balmy breeze.

The tuxedo was jet-black and might as well have been stitched to his body; it fitted like a second skin, emphasising the breadth of his shoulders and neatness of his waist.

She waited half a beat, giving him an opportunity to redeem the situation. It shouldn't be hard. He simply needed to offer a smile, or compliment her appearance, or ask about her day. She wasn't fussy. Any of the small ways a husband might greet his wife would have sufficed.

But instead Nikos looked at his wristwatch. 'Ready?'

She compressed her lips, the spark of mutiny colouring her complexion for a minute. 'Do I *look* ready?' she asked tartly, swishing past him and clipping across the room.

In the kitchen, she took two big sips of her champagne and then placed the glass down on the marble counter a little more firmly than she'd intended, so that a loud noise cracked through the room.

'Yes,' he said finally, closing the distance between them.

He stared down at her, his eyes flicking across the inches of her face. She didn't back away from him; she didn't let him see that her heart was being shredded by his lack of kindness. With her shoulders squared she walked ahead of him, out of the house and into the warm night air.

He opened the passenger door of the Ferrari for her and Marnie took her seat, careful not to touch him as she slid into the luxurious interior. The moment he sat beside her she was aware of his every single breath and movement. Unconsciously, she felt herself swaying closer to the window on her side, her eyes trained steadfastly on the view beyond the vehicle as they cruised away from his home.

At the bottom of the drive he turned left. Though Marnie was still getting her bearings, she'd ventured to the markets with Eléni enough times to know that he'd turned the car away from the city.

He drove without speaking, and she was glad of that. She needed the time to regain her composure, though she didn't have long. It was only a short distance to their destination: the ocean—and an enormous boat that was sparkling with the power of the thousands of tiny golden fairy lights that zigzagged across its deck. It was moored just off the coast.

'The party's on a boat?' she murmured, shifting to face him.

His eyes stayed trained on the cruise ship. 'As you see.'

She swallowed and bit back on a tart rejoinder. She'd vowed not to argue with him. Even that would show how she'd come to care too greatly. 'Great,' she snapped with acidity. 'I love boats.'

He was out of the car and rounding the side. Marnie pushed the door open and stepped out before he could reach her. After all, she'd opened her own doors all her life; why did that have to change now?

The ramp that led from the shore to the boat looked to have been specially constructed for the event. Though sturdy, it was obviously temporary. They were the only ones on it—though that was hardly surprising given that they were arriving well after the party had started.

'What is this *for*?' she asked as they stepped onto the polished deck.

'My bank throws it every year.'

'*Your* bank?' she clarified, pausing and turning to face him.

'The bank I work with,' he said distractedly. 'I do not own it.'

'I see.'

But from the second they arrived it became blatantly obvious that Nikos enjoyed an almost god-like status with the high and mighty of the institution.

Drinks were brought, food offered and advice sought.

Much of the conversation was in Greek or Italian, which Marnie understood only passably. She stood beside him listening, catching what she could, but her frustration was growing.

What was going on with him? He was acting as though she'd just knifed the tyres of his car or sold the secrets of their marriage to a tabloid. He was furious with her—and for what possible reason? She had done everything right! The clothes she wore, the hair, the make-up—she had put so much effort into being exactly what he needed of her that night. She was the picture-perfect tycoon's wife. And yet that seemed to have angered him.

When the group of men Nikos was deep in conversation with paused for a moment Marnie squeezed his arm. The smile on her face was broad; only Nikos would be able to detect the dark emotions that powered it.

'Excuse me a moment,' she murmured, pulling her hand away from him.

He bent down and whispered in her ear. 'Do you need something?'

'Yes.' She flashed her eyes at him in frustration, then encompassed his companions in her smile, knowing he wouldn't argue in front of them. 'Excuse me.'

She felt his eyes on her as she walked away, and just knowing that he was watching made her walk as though she hadn't a care in the world. Her feet seemed to glide over the deck, despite the crowds that were thick on the ground.

It was a perfect night. Sultry even though it was late in the summer season, and clear. The breeze was warm and soft, providing comfort rather than chill. She wove her way to the edge of the ship, seeking space and solitude. The polite smile on her face and a faraway look in her eyes discouraged conversation, and when she put her back to the crowds and stared out at the view she was all but absenting herself from the festivities.

She stood like that for a long time, enjoying the privacy of her thoughts, until a hand on her shoulder caught her attention.

Expecting to see Nikos, she masked her features with an expression of bland uninterest and turned slowly.

But the man opposite her caused such a flurry of feeling inside of her that tears welled instantly in her eyes.

'Anderson!' She hugged Libby's fiancé, her mind grappling with the question of why he was there even as she acknowledged how thrilled she was to see him. 'Oh! What a surprise.'

'I was hoping you'd be here.' He grinned. 'Nik wasn't sure you'd want to come.'

A frown briefly flashed in her face as she remembered that these two men were still close friends. Anderson was the one who had told Nikos about her father's dire situation, after all.

'Congratulations on the wedding.' He kissed her cheek, then grabbed two glasses of champagne from a passing waiter. 'To happily-ever-after, huh?' He clinked his glass to hers, earning a smile from Marnie.

'Indeed.' She drank the champagne, watching the man who would have become her brother-in-law over the rim of her glass.

'I wish I had been able to come to the wedding,' he said, nudging his hip against the railing and effectively screening them from the other guests.

Marnie studied him thoughtfully. Did he know what a farce their marriage was? 'I would have liked that,' she said finally, earning a laugh from Anderson.

'You sure? You sound ambivalent.'

She laughed, too. 'Sorry. I'm just surprised to see you. I somehow forgot that you and Nikos were close.'

His smile was warm. 'He's my oldest friend.'

Her heart turned over in her chest. She changed the

subject. 'I haven't seen you in a long time. You've been staying away from our house?'

He grimaced. 'I've been meaning to visit. But...'

'But?' she prompted, a smile belying any accusation.

'You know...I feel bad sometimes. Your parents look at me and see only Libby.' His smile was thin. 'I expect you know exactly what *that's* like.'

She sipped her champagne again, and her voice was carefully wiped of feeling when she spoke. 'It's not the same. They look at me and see only my failings as compared to Libby.'

Anderson rubbed a hand over his chin. 'They're wrong to compare the two of you. There's too many differences for it to make sense.'

Colour flashed in Marnie's cheeks. 'Thanks,' she said, with a hint of sarcasm.

'I wasn't being offensive,' he clarified quickly. 'Libby used to laugh and say that you and she were chalk and cheese. But that you were her favourite of all the cheeses in the world.'

Marnie's smile was nostalgic. 'I used to tell her that *she* was cheese and I was chalk. Doesn't that make more sense? She was sweet and more-ish and fair, and I'm a little...thin and brittle.' Her laugh covered a lifetime of insecurity.

'Don't *do* that,' Anderson said with frustration. 'She wouldn't want you to do that. She wasn't vain and she wasn't self-interested and she adored you. I know Arthur and Anne have always made you feel wanting, but that's not a true reflection. You owe it to Libby not to perpetuate that silliness.'

Marnie bit back the comments that were filling her mind. It was all too easy to justify her sense of inferiority, but with Anderson she didn't want to argue. 'I'm glad to see you,' she said finally.

'And I'm thrilled you and Nikos worked everything out. I know he never got over you.'

Marnie's eyes flew to Anderson's, confusion obvious in her features. Was it possible that even Anderson didn't know the true reason for their hasty wedding?

'Don't look so surprised,' Anderson said, sipping his drink. 'He might have played the part of bachelor to perfection but it was always you, Marnie. You're why he did all this.'

She shook her head in silent rejection of the idea, but Anderson continued unchecked. 'One night, not long after you guys broke up, he had far too much of my father's Scotch and told me that he'd earn his fortune and then win you back.'

'I can't imagine Nikos saying that.' But her heart was soaking in the words, buoying itself up with the hope that perhaps he *did* love her; that he *had* missed her.

'Oh, he talked about you all night. How you would only ever be serious about a guy like me. A guy with land and a title. He was determined to prove himself to you before he came back and won you over.' He laughed. 'If you ask me, he went a little far. I mean...a million would have done, right?'

Her smile was lacking warmth. She focussed her gaze on the gentle undulations of the water beneath the boat, her mind absorbing this information. 'It was never about money,' she said gently.

'Oh, I know that. I told him that a thousand times. But he didn't get it.' Anderson drained his champagne. 'Until you see first-hand the uniquely messed-up way Arthur and Anne made you girls feel you can't really understand a thing about you. Right?'

Startled, she spun to face him. Her breath was burning in her lungs and she wasn't sure what to say.

'You think you're the only one who had them in your

head? Libby almost didn't agree to marry me because she knew how *happy* it would make them. She was so sick of living up to their expectations that she said she wanted desperately to do the *wrong* thing—just once.'

'I can't believe it,' Marnie whispered, squeezing her eyes shut as she thought of Libby. 'She was the golden girl, and I never thought that bothered her.'

'It was a big mantle to wear,' he said simply.

Marnie expelled a soft breath and looked away. The breeze drifted some of her hair loose and she absentmindedly reached for it, tucking it back in place. 'I miss her so much,' she said finally.

Anderson was quiet for so long that Marnie wasn't sure he'd even heard her, or that she'd said the words aloud. Then, finally, he nodded and his voice cracked. 'Me, too.'

She wrapped her arms around him spontaneously, knowing that he understood her grief. That even years after losing Libby he stood before her a man as bereft now as he had been then.

From a distance they looked like a couple, he thought. The perfect blue-blooded pair. She with her couture gown and her swan-like neck angled towards Anderson's cheek. Her manicured hand resting on his hip, her flawless arm around his back.

His wife was beautiful, but in this environment, surrounded by Europe's financial elite, she was showcased to perfection—because she was at home. She was completely comfortable, whereas he felt the prestige like a knife in his side.

'If I did not trust you with my life I would be jealous of this little scene.'

Nikos's accented voice sent shivers of sensual awareness down Marnie's spine. She lifted away from Anderson, her eyes suspiciously moist. It caught Nikos's attention instantly. He looked from his wife to his friend, a frown on his face and a chasm in his chest.

'You are upset?'

She rolled her eyes. 'No. This is my happy face.'

He sent her a warning look that was somewhat softened when he reached into his pocket and removed a cloth handkerchief. She took it with genuine surprise at the sweetness of the gesture, dabbing at the corners of her eyes so as not to ruin her eye make-up.

'We were just reminiscing,' Anderson said simply.

Though he was subdued, he appeared to have largely regained control of his emotions.

'Your father was asking for you,' Nikos said to his friend.

'Bertram is here?' Marnie asked, a smile shifting her lips as she thought of the elder statesman. It transformed her face in an expression of such delicate beauty that Nikos had to stifle a sharp intake of breath.

'Yeah.' Anderson extended a hand and shook Nikos's. 'But I suspect your groom just doesn't want me monopolising you any longer.'

He winked at Marnie, obviously intending to make a swift departure.

She put a hand on his forearm to forestall him. 'Are you in Greece much longer? Will you come for dinner?'

'I'd love that,' Anderson said honestly. 'But we fly out tomorrow.'

Marnie's smile was wistful. 'Another time?'

'Sure.' He leaned forward and kissed her cheek, then winked at Nikos.

Alone with her husband, and the hundreds of other partygoers, Marnie felt her air of relaxation disappear. She reached for the railing, gripping it until her knuckles turned white. 'Are you having a good time?' she asked stiffly, her eyes seeking a fixed point on which to focus.

'It is good business for me to be here,' he said, lifting his broad shoulders carelessly.

'I wouldn't have thought your business required this sort of schmoozing.'

'That is true,' he said simply. 'But I do not intend to grow complacent in light of my success.'

She nodded, adding that little soundbite to the dossier of information she'd been building on him: *Nikos: V 2.0.*

This Nikos was determined to prove himself to the world—or was Anderson right? Was it that he wanted to prove himself to *her*? To prove that he deserved her?

No, that couldn't be it.

Had it not been for Arthur's financial ruin, Nikos would never have reappeared in her life.

'He might have played the part of a bachelor to perfection...' Anderson had said, and it had been an enormous understatement. Nikos had dedicated himself to the single life with aplomb. She'd lost count of the number of women he'd been reputed to be dating. And even 'dating' was over-egging it somewhat.

The women never lasted long, but that didn't matter. Each of those women had shared a part of Nikos that Marnie had been denied—a part that she'd denied herself.

Her eyes narrowed as she turned to study her husband. He'd followed her gaze and his eyes were trained on the mainland, giving her a moment to drink in his autocratic profile, the swarthy complexion and beautiful cheekbones that might well have been slashed from stone.

'Do you see that light over there?'

She followed the direction he was pointing in, squinting into the distance. There was a small glow visible in the cliffs near the sea. 'The hut?' she asked.

'Yes. It *is* a hut.' His sneer was not aimed at her; it showed agreement. He pinned her with his gaze; it was hard like gravel. 'That is where I spent the first eight years of my life.'

'Oh!' She resettled her attention on him, curiosity swelling in her chest, for Nikos had never opened up about his childhood even when they'd been madly in love. 'Is it?' She strained to pick out any details, but it was too far away. 'What's it like? Is it part of a town?'

'A town? No. There were four huts when I was growing up.' He gripped the railing tight. 'Two rooms only.'

She didn't want to say anything that might cause him to stop speaking. 'Did you like it?'

'*Like* it?' He lifted his lips in a humourless smile. 'It was a very free childhood.'

'Oh?'

'My father had a trawler. He came out here every day.'

'Squid?'

He nodded. 'Scampi, too.'

'You said you lived there until you were eight. What happened?'

He tilted his head to face her, his expression derisive. 'There was a storm. He died.'

'Nikos!' Sympathy softened her expression, but she saw immediately how unwelcome it was.

He shifted a little, indicating his desire to end the conversation.

'I should have told you he'd be here,' Nikos said only a moment later, surprising her with the lightning-fast change in conversation.

For a moment she didn't comprehend who he was talking about.

'It did not occur to me that Anderson would upset you.'

She drew her brows together in confusion. 'He didn't.'

'The tears in your eyes would suggest otherwise.'

She opened her mouth in an expression of her bemusement. 'This from the man who seems to live to insult me?' The words escaped before she could catch them.

Nikos nodded slowly, as if accepting her charge even

as his words sought to contradict it. 'Hurting you... That is not intentional. It is not what I want.'

She blinked and spun away, turning her body to face the railing. 'I can believe that.' And that hurt so much more! Knowing he could inflict pain without even trying, without even being conscious of her feelings, simply demonstrated how little he thought of her feelings at all.

'Do we have to stay long?' she asked, doing her best to sound unconcerned when emotions were zipping through her.

'No. Let's go. *Now.*'

He trapped her hand in his much bigger palm and led her from the party. Several times people moved to grab his attention, but Nikos apparently had a one-track mind, and it involved getting them off the boat.

At his Ferrari, with the moon cresting high in the sky and the strains of the party muffled by distance, Nikos put his hands on her shoulders and spun her to face him. His eyes seemed to tunnel into the heart of her soul.

'What is it I have done that's insulted you?'

She knew she couldn't deny it; after all, she'd just laid the charge at his feet. She shook her head, yet the words wouldn't climb to her tongue.

'Tell me, *agape...*'

'Nothing. It's fine.' Her eyes didn't meet his.

'Liar!' He groaned, crushing his mouth to hers.

His hands lifted, pulling at the pins that kept her hair in its chignon until they had all dropped to the ground in near-silent protest. He dragged his fingers through her hair, pulling at it and levering her face away.

His eyes bored into hers. 'I was angry with you tonight. I was rude.'

A sob was filling her chest. She wouldn't give in to it. '*Why?* What in the world could you have had to be angry about?'

Was that really her voice? With the exception of a slight tremor, she sounded so cool and in command! How was that possible when her knees were shaking and her heart was pounding?

'This. *You.*' He stepped backwards, as if to shake himself out of the hurricane of feelings. He pulled the door open and stared at her.

Marnie stared back. She wasn't going to let this go just because he appeared to have decided the conversation was at an end.

'What?' she demanded, lifting a hand and splaying her fingers against his broad chest. 'What *about* me? What did I do?'

'Do?' His head snapped back as if in silent revulsion. 'You did nothing. You cannot help that this is who you are.'

Her heart was pounding so hard now that it was paining her. 'I don't understand,' she said, with a soft determination that almost completely hid her wounds.

'No? Allow me to clarify. You are Lady Marnie Kenington and you always will be. You are this dress. This party. This perfect face. You are cold and you are exquisitely untouchable. The girl I thought I loved all those years ago never existed, did she?'

CHAPTER EIGHT

FOR THE FIRST time since her arrival in Greece the early morning was drenched by storm. The sky was leaden with weighty clouds, the ocean a turbulent, raging gradient of steel. White caps frothed all the way to the horizon, and the trees that marked the shore arched in the distance, folded almost completely in half.

Marnie, her knees bent under her chin, her eyes focussed on the ravaged horizon, took a measure of consolation from the destruction. Her mind, numb from the exhausting activity of trying to join the dots of what had happened the night before, looked for some kind of comparison in the wasted outlook.

The storm was trashing everything, and yet in time—perhaps even later that day—the clouds would disperse, the sun would shine, and all would look as it once had. Better, perhaps, for the rain had a spectacular way of cleaning things up, didn't it?

Could the same be said for her and Nikos?

Were they in the midst of a storm that would one day clear? Argument by argument, would they wash away their hurts?

She shook her head sadly from side to side, the question that had plagued her at length tormenting her anew.

Why had he married her?

'You are Lady Marnie Kenington and you always will be. The girl I fell in love with all those years ago never existed, did she?'

Had she?

He was right. Marnie had changed so much since then. He seemed to attribute it to her upbringing, to her parents' snobbery. Wasn't it more likely that she'd simply grown up?

She glanced down at her manicured fingernails and the enormous diamond that sparkled on her ring finger.

They were husband and wife, but outside of that, they were strangers. A lump formed in her throat; futility hollowed out her core.

He hadn't come to bed last night. She'd showered and waited for him—hoping, knowing, that their being together would make sense of everything. That when they made love the truth of their hearts was most obvious.

But she had no experience in the matter. Was it as he said? Just great sex? Or was it love? Or memories of love, like fragments of a dream, too hard to catch now in the bright light of reality and daytime?

She scraped her chair back impatiently. The pool was dark today, too, reflecting the sorrow of the skies. Had it been a stormy day like this when Nikos had lost his father? When the ocean had swallowed him up, perhaps as retribution for the fish he'd stolen out of its belly?

He had been silent and brooding on the car trip home, and Marnie had been too absorbed by his statement to try to break through that mood, to get to the heart of what he had meant.

Perhaps this morning they could talk.

She moved towards the kitchen, the thought of a cup of tea offering unparalleled temptation. And froze when she saw him.

It was like a flashback to the morning after they'd first

arrived. Impeccably dressed in a high-end business suit, he had his head bent over the newspaper and a cup to his left, which she knew would be filled with that thick coffee he loved.

'Good morning,' she murmured, her voice croaky from disuse.

He flicked a gaze to her face, studying her for one heart-stopping moment before smiling tightly and returning his attention to the paper.

So that was how it was going to be.

Marnie squared her shoulders and tipped up her chin defiantly. 'Did you sleep well?' She walked to the bench, standing directly opposite him.

Without looking up, he responded, 'Fine. And you?'

It was a lie. He hadn't got more than ten minutes altogether.

'Not really,' she said honestly.

He turned the page of the newspaper. Did she imagine that it was with force and irritation? The admission had cost her. It was an offer of peace—an acceptance of their relationship, faults and all.

'Where did you sleep?' she pushed, determined to crack through the facade he'd erected.

'In a guest room.' Still he read the damned newspaper.

Marnie, trying her hardest to forge past the storm, reached down and put her hand over the article. 'Nikos, we need to talk.'

He expelled a sigh and glanced at his watch. 'Do we?'

'You know we do.' She lifted her hand and moved it to his, lacing his fingers with her own. 'This isn't right.'

He moved his hand so that he could lift his coffee cup and drink from it. 'Talk quickly. I have a meeting.'

Hurt lashed her as a whip. 'That's not fair,' she said, with soft steel to her voice. 'You can't keep doing that.'

'Doing what?'

'Making yourself unavailable as soon as things get tough.'

'I relish obstacles. I relish difficult opportunities. But I cannot see the point in discussing anything with you right now.'

'So what you said last night isn't important enough to talk about?'

'What *did* I say?' he asked softly, his eyes roaming her face.

'Don't be fatuous,' she snapped. 'You made it sound like we didn't love each other. Like we didn't know each other.'

His look was one of confusion. 'But we *don't*.'

Denial! The sharpness of it plunged into her heart.

'I meant back then…' She limped the conversation along even when she felt as if she was dying a little.

'I said that the girl I thought I loved never existed,' he said with a shrug. 'That girl would have stood up for what we were. Would have fought to be with me. But you were never that. Seeing you last night, in that dress, you looked so perfect.' Derision lined his face. 'You've become exactly what your parents wanted.'

'You keep *doing* that! You keep making me out to be some kind of construct of theirs.'

'*Aren't* you?'

'Aren't we all?' she challenged. '*You* are a product of your life just as I am of mine. But if you hate me so much why the hell did you insist I marry you? It *has* to be more than revenge against my father'

He closed the paper and drained his coffee cup before placing it neatly on the edge of the sink. The seconds ticked by loudly in the background.

'Why do you think?'

A thousand possibilities clouded her mind, some of them dangling hope and others promising despair. 'I don't know,' she said finally, warily, shaking her head.

'To prove that I could have you.'

She had to brace her hands on the edge of the bench for support.

Her face flashed with such a depth of hurt that Nikos instantly wanted to call the words back. To defuse the situation and make her smile again. To make her laugh in that beautiful, inimitable way she had.

Laughter was a long way from Marnie's mind, though. 'You're serious?' She pressed her lips together, her mind reeling. 'This was just ego? As a seventeen-year-old I rejected you, and you couldn't handle that, could you? And now you've bullied me into this marriage so—what? So you can make me feel like this? So you can berate me and humiliate me...'

He held up a hand to silence her. 'I told you last night— I do not mean to hurt you. I never did.'

'Yeah, *right*.' She swallowed, her throat moving convulsively as she attempted to breathe normally. 'It didn't occur to you that this whole idea would hurt me?'

A muscle jerked in his cheek. 'Are you having regrets?'

'How can I *not* be? You put me in an impossible situation.' She spun away from him, looking out at the storm. She was at a crossroads. She could tell him the truth—that it was impossible to be married to him knowing he would never love her. Or she could remember that she *had* married him. A thousand and one reasons had driven her to it, and they were all still there.

Worse, Marnie stared down the barrel of her future and imagined it without Nikos and she was instantly bereft. Even this shell of a relationship, knowing he would share only a small part of himself with her, was better than nothing.

She'd faced life without him and it had been a sort of half-life. She'd poured all her energy into her work, and she'd dated men that she'd known her parents would approve of, but she hadn't felt truly alive until she'd seen Nikos once more.

Was it better to feel alive and permanently in pain or to be alone and feel nothing?

She turned to face him slowly, her face unknowingly stoic. 'I didn't hope for much from you, Nikos, but I expected at least that you would respect me. And do you know why? Because of who *you* are. Last night you said that the girl you fell in love with never existed. Maybe you feel that—maybe you don't. I don't know. But I have no doubt that I knew *you*. Who you were then. I think I know who you are now, too. And the contempt you are meeting me with is completely unwarranted.'

Her eyes sparked as she spoke the declaration.

'You say you married me to prove that you could have me. Well, I only married *you* to save my father. Did you honestly expect me to do anything less?'

'Not at all.' His voice was gravelly. 'You are excellent at taking direction.'

She sucked in a breath at the cruel remark. 'My parents were right to tell me to break it off with you. Not because you had no money or family prestige, but because you're a jerk.'

It wasn't funny but he laughed—a short, sharp sound of disbelief.

'I'm serious,' she said stiffly. 'I *am* Lady Marnie Kenington. I am the same woman I've always been. You forced me into this marriage and now you're angry with me just for being who I am. *You're* the one who's trying to make me something I'm not.'

Her words were little shards of glass, all the more potent for she was right. He couldn't fault her behaviour as his wife. She'd done and been everything he'd required of her. She hadn't shifted the goalposts—he had.

The realisation only worsened his mood. How could he

explain to her that he never enjoyed being at events like the party they'd attended the night before? That he hated most of the people in attendance, despised their grandiose displays of wealth and their desire to outdo one another. That he hated that entire scene and she was the very epitome of it? That seeing her amongst her own people—people who'd been born to wealth and prestige—made him realise that they'd never see the world the same way?

'You make an excellent point. I knew what I was getting when I suggested this marriage.' He looked at his wife long and hard. She was a woman who projected an image of being cool and untouchable—except with him. A gnawing sense of frustration engulfed him. 'Now, I really *am* late.'

He stalked towards the door, then turned back to face her. She was staring straight ahead with such an attempt at strength and resolve that something inside him twisted painfully.

'Marnie...' *What?* What could he offer her? 'We can make this work. The way we are in bed—'

'Is just great sex,' she reminded him, hating the words even as she spoke them.

But it was more than that. In bed, in his arms, Marnie was as he wanted her to be. Genuine, overflowing with desire and feeling: a real flesh-and-blood woman. Not the fancy ice queen she showed the world.

'Yes. And many marriages are built on less.'

'Great.' She appeared calm and in control, but her strength was crumbling. 'Don't you have a meeting to go to?'

He walked out of the door with a heavy pain in his gut that stayed with him all day.

His mind was shot. He lost concentration, he sent emails to the wrong people, he inverted figures on his spreadsheets.

He gave up on work in the early afternoon.

When he arrived home the place was deserted. He wandered from room to room, pretending he wasn't looking for Marnie, until he heard her voice drifting from the small space she'd claimed as her office.

By silent but mutual agreement he didn't intrude on her there. She generally only utilised it when he was at work, anyway. But curiosity drove him towards the door now, and he lingered for a moment on the threshold.

'We're in stage three of some very promising trials. Yes…'

She paused, and he could imagine the way she'd have that little line between her brows that showed deep concentration.

'That's true. Human trials are still a way off. But every day brings us closer.' Another pause. 'You're a gem, Mrs Finley-Johns. That's really very generous. Thank you.'

Silence filled the room for long enough that Nikos presumed she'd hung up the phone. He pushed the door inwards silently.

Marnie—his wife—was sitting at her desk, her honeyed hair piled into a messy bun, her head bent over a page as she handwrote something. He watched her for a moment and then stepped into the room.

That feeling in his gut didn't dissipate. He'd thought seeing her might do it. That just the sight of her might make everything slide back into place. It didn't.

When she realised she was no longer alone and lifted her gaze to his face he waited impatiently for a smile to burst sunshine through the room and relax his chest. It didn't. If anything, she was impatient, lifting her eyes to the clock above the door.

'Nikos? Is everything okay?' She reached for her phone, rotating it in her hands.

'Why do you ask?'

'It's so early,' she said with a look of confusion. 'You're usually not home for hours.'

He felt as if the ground was slipping beneath him. 'My afternoon was freed up,' he said with a shrug. 'You wanted to speak this morning and I rushed you. I thought we could go out for dinner and talk properly.'

The suggestion had come out of nowhere but as soon as he'd issued the invitation he'd known it was right.

'We did speak this morning.'

Their conversation had chased its way through her mind all day. Like a maze, it had twists and turns, but no matter which path she chased down they all finished in a dead end of despair.

'Not properly.' The words were gruff. He dragged a hand through his hair. 'Let's have dinner and try to be civilised.'

She arched a brow, genuine surprise obvious. 'I'm working.' She bit down on her lip. 'And I don't think anything's served by going out, do you?'

She sounded prim, and inwardly she winced. *'You'll always be Lady Marnie Kenington...'*

He crossed his arms over his chest, staring down at her. Marnie felt the imbalance in their arrangement and fought an urge to stand, to right it. That would just be symbolic; the true imbalance would remain.

'What is it you are doing? For work?' His smile was an attempt to relax her. To elicit a similar reaction in her. It failed. 'Or is it still a secret?'

'It's not a secret.' She shook her head. 'It never has been. I do behind-the-scenes fundraising for a cancer charity. Specifically leukaemia research.'

It wasn't what he'd expected and that was obvious. He rubbed a hand over his stubbled chin, propping his hip against the doorframe. He was settling in. Marnie swallowed. Her insides were clenching with desire, her mind was sore from trying to figure out what the hell they were doing, and all she could think as she looked at him was how much she wanted him. To hell with everything else.

'Why behind the scenes?'

She blinked, passing her phone from one hand to the other. 'It's more my thing.'

'I would have thought your profile would garner donations...'

'My name does that, too.' She shrugged, placing the phone down on the desk and clasping her hands together in her lap. 'And my contacts.'

He took a step into the office, looking at the computer screen. It had a list of names with donations beside them, tracking various contributions for the last few years.

'You are apparently very effective at this,' he murmured, leaning forward and scrolling down the page.

His body framed hers, trapping her within the circle of his arms. She thought of telling him to stop looking, saying that her work was confidential. But why? Nikos Kyriazis was hardly likely to be indiscreet with the information, and most of her donors released details of their charitable contributions as a way of attracting good publicity.

'Thanks,' she said, allowing herself to extract a small kernel of pleasure from his praise. 'I suppose it's because I feel passionately about it.'

'Yes...' He straightened, but stayed where he was, so that his legs straddled hers. 'How come you have not asked *me* to donate?'

Her smile was a twist of her pink lips. 'You don't think you've donated enough to my cause already?'

That feeling in his gut intensified in a burst of pain. 'This is different.'

She shook her head. 'Not really.' She ran a fingernail over the hem of her skirt, drawing his attention to her smooth, tanned legs.

'Why don't we go for dinner and you can tell me about this? Your charity. Pretend I am a donor you want to win over.'

'But you're not,' she said with a shake of her head. 'And I don't want to ask you to put money into this.'

'It matters so much to you, though,' he pointed out logically. 'Surely you wouldn't turn me down?'

She shrugged, perfecting an air of impatient unconcern. 'If you want to donate, you can. That's your business.'

'Tell me more about it first.'

Marnie bit down on her lip, her eyes drifting to his face. The time she'd spent in an attempt to make sense of their situation had all been a waste, for here was yet another facet of Nikos Kyriazis that wholly renewed the riddle. His ability to set aside their contretemps and the harsh words he'd issued made her head spin.

She nodded finally, expelling a soft sigh. 'Fine. We'll talk at dinner.'

Nikos had dismissed enough people enough times in his life to know that he was being dismissed from her office. Feeling that somewhere in their conversation he'd scored a minor victory, he didn't push it.

CHAPTER NINE

In England, Marnie was used to being recognised. She hated the sensation but she'd come to expect it, so she had long ago given up the idea of eating in glamorous high-profile restaurants without expecting to be photographed and approached by all and sundry.

In Athens it was Nikos who drew the long, speculative glances. Nikos whose name opened doors and inspired attention and curiosity.

Marnie was actually enjoying being an outsider to the sense of celebrity. She'd never craved it, and watching him being fawned over by waitresses and even the manager at the exclusive Athens hot spot from the moment they arrived brought a small smile to her lips now.

He saw it immediately. Of their own volition his eyes dropped to the curve of her pink mouth and fire warmed her belly.

'Yes, Marnie?' he prompted, leaning forward so that a hint of his masculine fragrance teased her nostrils, making her gut clench with unmistakable desire. She tried to ignore it.

She crossed her legs beneath the table and shrugged. 'I was just thinking how nice it is that I'm unknown here.'

'Not unknown,' he said, with a small shake of his head.

'Well, *lesser* known,' she corrected. 'Less relevant. And you're…'

'Yes?' He broke off the query when a waitress appeared with a bottle of ice-cold champagne.

'Compliments of the owner.' She smiled at Nikos, her cleavage exposed as she leaned forward to pour some of the liquid into a long, tapered flute.

'Thank you,' he murmured dismissively. 'You were saying…?'

Marnie waited for the waitress to finish pouring. 'You're who everyone wants to see.' She grinned. 'I'm anonymous and you're hot property.'

His laugh surprised her. It was rich and warm, and reminded her of how long it had been since she'd heard the sound.

'Hot property?' He shook his head. 'I'm glad to hear you think so.'

'You know what I mean.' Colour bloomed in her cheeks. She focussed on the menu. 'What's good here? What do you recommend?'

'It is all excellent.' He shrugged.

She scanned the menu but she was far from hungry. Butterflies had taken up residence in her stomach and their beating wings made it impossible for her to imagine accommodating food into their kaleidoscope.

'What do you suggest?'

His eyes narrowed. 'I can order for you, if you'd like?'

'That won't be necessary.' She shut down his perfectly normal offer, knowing how dire it would be to keep conceding to him.

'As you wish.' He pushed the menu away, his mind apparently made up.

She continued to skim her eyes over the words on the page but they were puddles and blurs.

'How long have you done this work?'

She started, despite the fact his suggestion of dinner had been hung on a desire to learn more about the trust.

'About four years,' she said, reaching for the stem of her champagne flute simply for something to do.

'You didn't go to university?'

She shook her head. 'The timing wasn't right.'

A frown smudged his handsome face. 'In what way?'

Marnie pulled her lower lip between her teeth and Nikos surprised her by reaching over and abruptly swiping his thumb across her mouth, disturbing the gesture.

'Don't think.' He spoke commandingly, his words gravelled. 'You do this too often.'

Her expression was blank. 'I wasn't aware thinking was a crime.'

'It is when you are selecting which words to use to your husband. Just answer my questions directly.'

Marnie gaped, her mouth parted on an exhalation of surprise. 'That hardly seems fair.'

'Why was the timing not right?' He returned to his original question, impatient for an answer.

He was right. She *had* been prevaricating, unconsciously trying to select words that wouldn't apportion blame or imply resentment.

'I wasn't ready to leave home,' she said quietly.

But he understood what she hadn't been willing to say. 'You mean your parents didn't want you to go?' His disapproval was marked, despite the way he spoke quietly.

The waitress reappeared, her smile bright. Was it also inviting? Or was Marnie being paranoid?

She flicked her gaze back to the menu, intent on seeming not to notice the way the waitress lingered a little too close to Nikos as she spoke.

Nikos didn't appreciate the interruption, and his annoyance brought a childish kernel of pleasure to Marnie. She hesitated over ordering for far longer than was necessary, finally selecting scampi followed by chicken, having changed her mind several times.

Nikos glared at her and spoke in Greek, quickly dispensing with the waitress.

'They forbade you from attending university?'

She started, shaking her head softly so that her hair flew around her cheeks. 'Not at all.'

'You wanted to study law. You were passionate about it.'

'Not really.'

He ignored the rejoinder. After all, they'd spent a long time talking about their hopes and dreams. He had not misunderstood her desire to go into law. Nor did he doubt she would have achieved the requisite grades.

'But instead you stayed at home, living with your parents, working for a charity that revolves around your sister's illness,' he murmured, with a directness she hadn't expected.

'Do you think there's something wrong with that?'

'Yes.' He leaned forward and put his hand on hers. 'You are a person, too, Marnie. You are not simply Libby's sister. Nor your parents' daughter. You have your own life to live.'

She compressed her lips and pulled her hand down to her lap. 'You say that even after blackmailing me into this marriage?'

She sipped her champagne but it was too sweet. She didn't want it. She was definitely not in the mood to celebrate. She ran her finger around the rim, staring at the hypnotic, frantic movement of the bubbles as her mind spun over the situation they found themselves in.

'It's not as if I can't move on,' she said quietly, her eyes refusing to meet his. 'But without funds research into leukaemia is slow. It occurred to me that the people most likely to succeed at raising money are probably those who have every reason to passionately pursue it. In ten years— who knows? Maybe girls like Libby won't get sick.'

Finally, she forced herself to lance him with her eyes; they were softened by sorrow.

'It's idealistic, but...'

He surprised her by murmuring, 'Not at all. You are right. Progress does not always happen as you expect it to. Sometimes it is hard-fought, and other times it is over-night, as though a cascade of discoveries slides into place. But without funds neither is likely.'

She nodded, distracted enough by the subject matter to speak naturally. 'I thought I'd do it for a year. As a way of giving back to the trust that was so supportive to us. But it turns out I sort of have a knack for it.'

'I can imagine,' he said. 'Do you regret not studying law?'

It was on the tip of her tongue to deny it, but the truth came to her first. 'Yeah. Sometimes. But that would have been about helping people, too. I'm just helping different people now.'

He let the words sink in and shied away from the in-trinsic guilt they evoked. After all, her propensity to help others was what had made it impossible for her to walk away from his marriage proposal.

'And staying at home instead of finding your own place...?'

Her smile was enigmatic. 'You know... Kenington Hall is enormous. I have my own wing. It's much like living on my own.'

'And your parents are your neighbours?' he murmured, his voice ringing with disbelief.

'Yes.' She nodded. 'But apparently I'm a pretty inatten-tive neighbour,' she said with regret. 'I had no idea about Dad's troubles.'

His desire to comfort her displeased him. 'I imagine he was adept at concealing the truth.'

'Not really.' She shook her head wistfully.

The waitress appeared with their starters, placing them on the table and then disappearing without a word. Marnie wondered if Nikos had commanded her to stop making conversation when he'd switched to speaking Greek earlier.

Nikos watched as Marnie lifted her fork and speared a single scampi. She put it down again almost instantly, and when she looked at him he felt a wave of guilt emanating from her.

'I should have seen the signs.'

'What signs?' he prompted.

'He's been stressed. Angry. He's just not himself.'

Nikos found it hard to find any genuine sympathy for the man, but he realised he didn't like seeing Marnie suffer. *At all.* 'Tell me something...'

She nodded, toying with her fork.

'After your father paid me off, were you angry with him?'

Marnie's eyes flashed with emotion. 'I didn't know about that, remember?'

He waved a hand dismissively through the air. 'Fine. After I left, were you angry with him? With your mother?'

'I...' She shuttered her eyes closed, her dark lashes fanning over her translucent cheek.

'Do not *think*!' He repeated his earlier directive and she grimaced.

'I was furious,' she said, so quietly he had to lean forward to catch the words. 'But they're my parents, and they'd been through so much.' She swallowed. 'My father threatened...' She closed her mouth on the threat she'd been about to repeat. 'My father was devastated by losing Libby.'

'And he threatened you?' Nikos prompted, with a smoothness that spoke of determination.

She thought about lying. But wasn't there so much water under the bridge now?

'They made me choose.'

The anticlimax brought about in him an intense sense

of disappointment. Right when he'd thought he might finally be going to understand just what had led to Marnie pushing him far, far away, she'd gone back to the old lines.

'I mean they *literally* told me they'd disown me if I didn't break it off with you,' she added with a look of grief on her beautiful features.

She was back in the past, her mind far from him in that moment.

'I didn't care when they said they'd disinherit me.' She looked at him—and through him. 'Money meant nothing to me. But they were my link to Libby, and they said they wouldn't have me in their lives so long as I was with you. That I would never be allowed to return to Kenington Hall.' Marnie's voice cracked. 'The house was—is—all I have left of her...'

Marnie woke with a start as the plane pitched a little in one direction. She'd dozed off, despite the fact their flight had been a morning one. She stifled a yawn with the back of her hand, her groggy eyes drifting to her husband's bent head.

He was working.

A smile flicked to her lips with ease, though her stomach churned with a mix of anxiety and an emotion that was so much more confusing.

She didn't have time to attempt to understand it before the plane shuddered and Marnie's panic overtook everything. She dug her fingernails into the armrests, her expression showing distress.

Nikos, attuned to her every move, looked up instantly. 'There is thick cloud-cover over London, that's all.'

She nodded, but her childhood fear of flying was ricocheting through her. Marnie stared out of the window, trying to distract herself with thoughts of her father's birthday weekend—anything to curtail the clear picture she had in her mind of the aeroplane spearing nose-first towards the earth.

Their trip had come round quickly—for Marnie, almost too quickly.

After that one night in Athens when they'd shared dinner she felt as if a new understanding had settled between her and her husband and she wanted to hold on to that, to strengthen the understanding that was building between them. Would a trip back to her parents' unsettle the bridge they'd been building?

They were not a normal couple.

There was no shared love between them—at least not on Nikos's part. Perhaps not on Marnie's part either.

She had spent a great deal of her energy trying to decipher and separate her feelings of lust from love; her feelings of past love from present infatuation. Some days she convinced herself that she'd fallen in love with only the *idea* of Nikos—an idea that bore only a passing resemblance to the ruthless, determined businessman he'd become.

But then he would do something sweet—like bringing her tea in bed when she'd slept late, or calling in the middle of the day to remind her of something small they'd discussed the night before—and her heart would flutter and her soul would know she loved him. Not in a sensible, rational way, but in the way that love sometimes bloomed even when it was not watered or fed.

They barely argued. By tacit agreement each tried to respect the other's limitations. Marnie accepted the dark streak that ran through Nikos—the side of him that was so hell-bent on making her father see how wrong he was to have passed Nikos off as a failure that he'd blackmailed her into marriage. If she thought about it too much it made her queasy, so she pushed it to the recesses of her mind and clung to a sort of blind hope. Maybe one day he wouldn't feel that aching resentment so forcefully?

Their truce was underpinned by a sex life that made her toes curl. He had been right about that. Even if it was all they had to go on it would make their marriage worth staying in. Wouldn't it?

But uncertainty lurked just beyond her acceptance. For they had travelled stormy waters, and weren't there always eyes in storms? The calm that gave a moment's respite before the intensity of the cyclone returned with twice its strength?

Was she in the eye of a storm?

Or was this a lasting peace?

Only time would tell, and Marnie had a lifetime to wait and see.

CHAPTER TEN

THE APPLE WAS as sweetly sun-warmed as those she remembered from childhood. Despite the fact the day was cool, the morning had offered just enough heat to darken the flesh of this one more than the others.

Though it wasn't yet midday, she was tired. They'd been travelling since dawn and the return to Kenington with Nikos by her side had brought with it a sledge-load of emotions.

Juice dribbled down one side of her mouth and she lifted a finger to catch it.

Nikos watched, transfixed.

'I used to love coming down here to the apple orchard...'

'I remember.'

Memories. They were his problem. They were thick in the air around them. Memories of how it had felt then. When he'd been young and in love. He would have plucked a matching apple from another branch and enjoyed its fruity flesh alongside Marnie.

She stopped walking and turned around, her back to the heavily adorned fruit trees. 'I always think this is the best aspect of the house.' She lifted her free hand and framed the building between her forefinger and thumb. Her smile was born of whimsy. 'Until I go to the rose garden or Libby's garden. Then I think *that* view is preferable.'

She crunched into the apple once more.

'Perhaps it is the same from all viewpoints,' he suggested, with a hint of cynicism that was out of place and sounded, even to his own ears, forced.

'Maybe.' She shrugged and began to walk back towards the house.

He resisted the urge to ask her to stay with him where they were a little longer.

'Thank you for coming with me this weekend.'

His laugh was short. 'I presumed my attendance wasn't optional.'

She lifted her face to his. 'I would think almost *everything* is optional for you.'

His smile was without humour—a relic of his twisted laugh. 'Not this.'

She didn't pretend to misunderstand. 'When are you seeing him?'

'We're meeting after lunch.'

Marnie stopped walking, reaching for Nikos's hand. Her fingers curled around his as though they belonged. Familiarity and comfort knotted through her, momentarily putting aside the nausea and anxiety that had besieged her since they'd arrived in London.

'What is it, *agape*?'

A husky question. A promise, too, laced with so many emotions she couldn't translate.

'You know how stubborn he is?'

Nikos's lips curled. 'Yes.'

'I just don't know if he'll let you help. And I'm… I'm scared.'

His eyes held hers, probing her, trying to read her soul. 'Tell me something, Marnie. Why do you care?'

She started, scanning his face. But Nikos wasn't backing off. In fact, he moved closer, welding his body to hers, linking his arms behind her back. His nearness was seductive and distracting.

'Besides the fact he's my father?'

'Blood isn't everything. Your parents don't seem too concerned with your happiness. You're not close to them.'

'Of course I am,' she said with a shake of her head.

He laughed, dismissing her assertion easily. 'You don't speak to them. You don't speak *of* them—except with a sense of obligation and guilt because you survived and Libby died.'

She was startled at his perceptiveness.

'You married a man who saw you only as a means of revenge in order to stave off the financial fate that they deserve.'

'They're my *parents*,' she mumbled, her eyes flicking closed. The pain of his words was washing through her. 'And I'm very grateful to you.'

'Grateful?' He stepped backwards, shaking his head. '*Thee mou.* You offer me *gratitude*? I tell you I see you as a means of revenge and you say thank you?'

She frowned. 'You know what I mean.'

'No, I don't. You have been pushed around by your parents, and by me, and yet you seem to treat us all with civility and thankfulness. I cannot comprehend this.'

She swallowed. 'Do you need to?'

He shook his head. 'No.' He lifted a hand to her cheek and stroked it. 'And I suppose the same could be said for you.'

She pressed a hand to his chest, perhaps intending to put some distance between them, but the warmth of him, the beating of his heart, was mesmerising.

'Do you really believe our marriage comes down to revenge and sex?'

'Our marriage—' He began to speak, the words thick with meaning. He stared into her eyes; he was drowning in them. They were the depths to her soul; the truth to her questions. They mirrored his past, his heart and all his hopes.

They were beautiful eyes. How could people mistake her for being cold-hearted? In her eyes there was always a twisting of emotion and thought, of kindness and concern. Yet he had missed it. He had believed her unfeeling and incapable of true emotion at one point. He'd clung to that; he'd enjoyed believing it of her.

'Yes?'

It was a husk. An invitation for him to say something that would smooth away the pain of their predicament. A contradiction of the fact that he had bought her out of a need to avenge past wrongs.

But they were wrongs he'd carried with him for a long time. Was he willing to let them go? And, if so, what did that mean?

'Marnie?'

The voice was shrill and imperious, cutting across the lawn and breaking through the growing understanding that had been forming between them. He was unwilling to close their conversation, but a cloud instantly seemed to spread across Marnie and she stepped back.

The woman who had pulled a sweet apple from a frothy tree and crunched into it hungrily was gone. Lady Heiress was his companion now—only her eyes showed that Marnie was still in there.

'It doesn't matter,' she said quietly, shifting her gaze to the manor house in the background. 'I'm glad you're going to help him. Only be gentle, Nikos. And...' She turned to face him, hurrying now as Anne Kenington approached them. 'I know you said *you* would decide if you wanted to tell him the truth about our arrangement but...'

It seemed like an age ago that they'd had that conversation, but it had only been a month! Something strange lodged in her mind—a recollection she couldn't quite grab so she pushed it aside.

'But could you not? Not this weekend? I know you hate him, and that it's tempting to throw it in his face. But not now. Please?'

He stared at her without speaking and Marnie continued anxiously.

'I don't think I could forgive that. It would be... It really would be the end of what we used to mean to one another.'

Nikos was perplexed—and something else. Something he couldn't analyse or comprehend. So he spoke honestly. 'I have no intention of telling your father you married me to clear his debts.'

'Don't say that!'

She was visibly stricken, but Anne was almost upon them. Like a consummate professional Marnie blinked and slid her mask into place.

It annoyed him, and he wanted to prise it off again—just for a moment. He was sick and tired of masks and pretence.

'It's the truth,' he replied softly, clinging to that fact for her sake as much as his own.

Did he want her to contradict him? Did he want her to redefine their marriage? How could he expect that of her? A challenge? A gauntlet? One he knew she'd never answer.

'Isn't it?'

Their conversation had left Nikos in a foul mood. The lack of resolution, the constant chasing one another in circles, had given him the feeling that as soon as he began to comprehend a facet of his wife she morphed into something else and slipped out of his grip and downstream from him completely.

Worse was the sense that he was losing his own convictions in the face of hers. To lose one's sister would be hard enough, but to have your parents threaten to cut you completely from their life and support... Even Marnie, who had always seemed to have certainty and strength to her, must have been terrified of what that would mean.

How *dared* they? How had they dared to speak to their own child with such cold disregard?

It was not the ideal mind-set to bring to his meeting with Arthur Kenington. Nor was it the ideal backdrop. This study of Arthur's was familiar, yet different. Since they'd stood here six years earlier many changes had taken place—not least between the two men.

The walls were filled with a collection of books, impressive volumes that had never been thumbed—perhaps carefully selected by an interior designer who had chosen the titles because they would add *gravitas* to a man who was otherwise lacking in it—there was an elegant liquor tray that looked to be well-used, and a family photograph that was framed above Arthur's desk.

Arthur and Anne had barely aged, though Libby and Marnie looked much younger, so the picture must have been taken at least a decade earlier.

Arthur caught Nikos's gaze and grimaced. 'Our last family photo. We used to get them done every year until... we lost her.' He coughed, his slight paunch wobbling a little with the involuntary spasm. 'It didn't make much sense after that.'

Nikos didn't respond. Marnie and Libby stood at the foreground of the photo, Libby's arm wrapped around her sister's shoulders. There was an air of genuine affection between the girls: a sign of true camaraderie. Perhaps it had developed as a result of this environment?

'She was such an angel,' Arthur continued, perhaps misunderstanding Nikos's interest. 'Not a girl in the world like her.'

Nikos felt a possessive protective instinct flash in his gut. Yes, Libby had been lovely. And beautiful in a way that was ordinary and common. Unlike Marnie, with her steely, watchful gaze and determined little chin. Her reserve that made it difficult for her to speak to people unless she really, truly admired them.

'We need to discuss your business,' Nikos said sharply, not wishing to wander down Arthur's Libby-paved Memory Lane a moment longer. 'My information on your situation has me...concerned.'

'And what information is that?'

Nikos leaned forward, bracing his elbows on his thighs. 'It is no secret. You are out of immediate danger, but that is only temporary.'

'I don't believe that.'

'Then you are a fool.' Nikos spoke sharply.

Six years had passed since their last private conversation, and in that time Nikos had become used to having the world obey him. Deference generally met his commands—not dithering indecision.

'Do you want to lose it all, Arthur?'

'Of course I don't. But it won't come to that. Mark my words, there'll be—'

'Nothing.' Nikos eased back in his chair. 'You are overcommitted. There are no more assets left to shore your interests up and the market continues to fluctuate wildly. I am your only chance.'

The silence sparked between them. It was electrified by resentment.

'You're enjoying this, aren't you?'

Nikos didn't pretend to misunderstand; his smile was thin and unknowingly filled with disparagement. 'How I feel isn't relevant,' he said finally.

Strangely, he wasn't enjoying it. He had spent a long time imagining a situation like this. How good it would feel to throw his own success in Arthur Kenington's face. A man who had told him he would never amount to anything! He'd fantasised about it, and he'd done everything he could—even sacrificing his conscience—to achieve this moment.

And he felt nothing. Except, perhaps, a pervasive pity for this man who had let vanity and arrogance get in the way of financial security. His voice was softer when he spoke again, conciliatory.

'You cannot lose your business. Nor this house. It would devastate Marnie.'

'Marnie?' A scoff of surprise. 'She'd recover. This place never meant to her what it did to Libby.'

Nikos's fingers flexed into a fist on his lap, but he kept his face impassive. How was it possible that her own father understood her so little? Did he not see what she didn't say? Didn't he understand that her reticence to express emotions didn't mean that she lacked them?

'It is for Marnie's sake that I offer my assistance, so do not disdain her feelings.'

The statement held a barely contained warning. Nikos, though, knew he had no option *but* to help. It was a promise he had made to Marnie and he would never break it.

Arthur dragged a hand through his hair, his eyes skidding about the room. 'There has to be a way...'

'Yes. There is. *I'm* it. You know I have the money. A single phone call would remove this worry from your life.'

'You have the money?' Arthur spat, his eyes glistening with dark rage. '*You.* A boy I all but dismissed as—' He had the wisdom to cut the sentence off.

'Yes?' Nikos demanded through bared teeth.

'Worthless.' Arthur spat the word with satisfaction.

Nikos stood, his powerful stride taking him to the window. He looked down on Libby's garden and imagined Marnie there. His will strengthened. The papers he'd had couriered to him that morning were heavy in his pocket, begging for attention.

'You were wrong.' He turned, his eyes pinning Arthur where he sat. 'Do you want my help or not?'

A long silence clouded them. Nikos studied his opponent—there was no mistaking the adversarial nature of their relationship in that moment. With no one else to witness their interaction both men had dropped their masks of civility.

'I offer it to you with only one condition.'

Arthur snorted. 'I knew it was too good to be true.'

'Perhaps.' Nikos nodded, knowing for certain now the only way he could make sure Marnie was well-looked-after for the rest of her life. 'But it is your only chance to salvage something of your pride, so I suggest you listen.'

'The gloves are off, eh?' Arthur snapped, but there was weariness in his defiance.

'If the gloves were off you would know about it,' Nikos contradicted. 'The terms of my helping you are to stay between us. Marnie need never know what we have discussed here. Understood?'

Was it any wonder that, hours later, surrounded by formally dressed party guests, Arthur Kenington stayed as far from Nikos as possible? His concessions that afternoon had been hard-fought and potentially confidence-destroying. Evidently he found the idea of celebrating his birthday with his son-in-law impossible to contemplate.

Nikos didn't mind. In fact he barely noticed. Making Arthur eat crow had offered him no satisfaction, and yet he'd thought about the moment for years. How odd that once he'd had the chance to make the man beg for help he'd skated over it and provided assistance on a silver platter instead.

He considered the matter with Arthur closed. He didn't intend to think of it again save for one salient point that would require delicate handling. Would Marnie be angry when she discovered the exact nature of his help? Would she resent what he'd done?

His entire focus shifted to her. He watched her speaking to her parents' friends with the effortless grace that had first captivated his attention. Holding a glass of Scotch cradled in the palm of his hand, he felt the full force of that long-ago afternoon swarm through him.

He had come to Kenington Hall reluctantly. Spending time with Anderson and Libby had tended to leave him feeling like a third wheel, and yet Anderson had been so welcoming to him. He had been the one guy at school who *hadn't* seen Nikos as an outsider, and Nikos had repaid his friendship with unswerving loyalty. So when Anderson had asked Nikos to tag along he'd put aside his own reticence and travelled to the estate of one of England's noble families.

And he'd met Marnie.

She'd been seventeen and utterly breathtaking.

'Don't go near the horses. They're in a foul mood today!'

She had laughed as she'd torn past him, her long hair flowing behind her, the horse moving too quickly to catch more than a passing glimpse. Yet she'd reminded him of a sort of young Boadicea. Beautiful and strong, striking and confident, full of life and vitality.

Had he loved her from that moment? He'd certainly been fascinated.

'Hi.'

Her voice came to him now as if from a long way away. He lifted his head, capturing her in his gaze. But that moment was still around him and before he could question the wisdom of it he smiled at her as though they were back in that time, just Nikos and Marnie, without all the subsequent heartbreak.

She felt the purity of his look and it rang through her,

but she'd been worrying all afternoon and the habit was hard to break. 'Did you speak to him?'

He nodded, his stubborn smile still on his features.

Her hair had caught the sunshine as she'd gone past him that day. It had been like gold. He reached for it now and flicked the ends, bringing his body close to hers. She smelled good. Like apples and desire.

'And...?' Her eyes skimmed his, but her breath was coming fast and hard, making her breasts lift and fall.

'And what?' he prompted, wrapping his arms around her waist.

The band was playing a slow jazz song, the singer crooning gently into the elegant space. The formal dining room was large, and it had been converted into a ballroom for the purpose of tonight. Enormous flower arrangements punctuated the walls at regular intervals.

'Did you...?' She looked around, conscious of their surroundings.

'Yes?' he drawled, though he knew where she was going.

'Did you fix it?'

'Well, I couldn't transfer a hundred million pounds to your father in one afternoon,' he murmured sardonically, 'but, yes, *agape*. He has agreed to accept my help.'

She let out a whoosh of relief and he studied her features thoughtfully.

'You thought he might refuse? Even now?'

She shrugged, her shoulders slim and pale. 'I don't know. Like I said, he's stubborn.'

'You don't need to worry about it any more,' he said gently.

'I know.' She smiled up at him. 'Am I allowed to thank you now?'

'No.' He drew her closer, so that she could feel the strength of his body.

'Why not?'

'My helping him was entirely self-serving. You don't owe me thanks.'

She rested her cheek against his chest, listening to the beating of his strong heart. 'Was he grateful?' she asked instead, changing tack slightly.

His laugh was quiet but she felt it rumble through him.

'He was incensed.'

She grimaced. 'It wouldn't have been easy for him to face you, knowing what a mess his interests are in.'

'No,' Nikos conceded, without feeling the need to point out that Arthur only had himself to blame.

'I don't care.' She looked up at him. 'I'm going to thank you, anyway. How can I not?'

He stared down at her familiar face and the past blurred with the present. 'Fine. Then I can tell you how I wish you to express your gratitude.'

'Yes?' she murmured, her stomach swirling.

'For this night let's not speak about your family. Nor our past. We have spent a month retracing it and I wonder if we'll ever understand one another. Tonight I just want to dance with my wife. To kiss her. To feel her body. To be here with her and not think about the reasons we married. Deal?'

Hope blew open inside her. Surely that spoke of wanting a fresh start—of believing they were worthy of one. She looked at him for a long moment and knew exactly what it was that danced with hope.

Love.

Love for *him*.

Despite everything he'd done to get her into his life, she felt fierce love burst through her. It was not born of gratitude. Nor circumstances. It was the same love she'd always felt for him, only stronger—because it had been scorched by life, loss and disappointment and still it was there.

She stood up on tiptoe and pressed her lips lightly to his. 'Deal.'

The next song was another indistinct jazz tune. The singer's voice was low and husky and they danced slowly, in the middle of the crowd but aware only of each other. Marnie breathed in time with him, her eyes whispering shut, every fibre of her being in sync with her husband. So that when he stopped dancing and dropped his arms to his sides, capturing one of her hands in the process, and began to move towards the large glass doors, Marnie went with him without question.

'Do you know what I was thinking about today?' he asked as they emerged to see the moon casting a silver string from the inky sky above.

'Other than the significant hit your finances are about to take?' she offered with a teasing smile.

'Other than that.' He guided her along the terrace towards a small courtyard he'd seen earlier that day.

'What?'

'I was remembering the first time I met you.'

Marnie's heart was thunder; Nikos was lightning.

'Yes...?' Her voice was a husk.

He moved towards a balustrade, reclining against it with an expression that Marnie couldn't fathom.

'Being back here with you makes it feel like yesterday.'

And yet it wasn't. It was far in the past, with no way of recapturing that time. They could only exist in the moment. What they were now had to sustain them. The past would never be enough.

'I thought we weren't going to talk about our history,' she said with an uncertain smile.

'You're right.'

Marnie closed the distance between them as though a magnetic field was drawing her to him. She stood in front of him, the moon dancing across her face, a small smile on her lips.

'So let's talk about now.' She dared herself to be brave. To look at him with all her hope and want. 'Do you still think that we're just about sex?'

'And revenge,' he murmured, but an answering smile was playing about his lips and it surged her sense of hope higher.

'Of course.' She copied his expression, her look droll. 'Well, if it's meaningless sex you're after, that's fine by me.'

His laugh was warm butter on her frazzled nerves. 'I'm glad to hear it, Mrs Kyriazis.'

His fingers traced the bare skin of her arms and she shivered involuntarily. Anticipation trembled inside her. He caught her hand in his and together they walked. Was he leading her? Or the other way around? Marnie couldn't have said.

They went to the room that had been hers as a child. In the distance, the sounds of merriment could be heard. Wine glasses chinking, music, conversation. But it was all far away from where they were. Their world was their own, their breathing and needs the only noise.

She slipped into the room ahead of him, turning around in time to see him click the door shut and press the ancient lock down. His hands were lifting to his tie, loosening it in one movement so that it hung around his neck, a stunning black contrast to the sharp whiteness of his shirt.

Marnie reached for the zip on her dress, tucked under her arm, but a simple shake of Nikos's head stilled her.

'Let me,' he murmured, stalking towards her with a look she couldn't quite understand.

His face was set in a mask of *something*, and that something made her heart hammer in her chest.

'Let me,' he repeated, though she'd offered no opposition. Was he asking for something else? The air felt heavy with unuttered words, but perhaps they were all inside her.

She swallowed, the fragile column of her neck shifting with the movement. His fingers at her side were gentle, pulling at the zip so that she felt the slow whisper of cool air against her flesh. Goose bumps rioted across her and she drew in a sharp breath as he lowered the dress with a reverence she hadn't imagined possible. Standing before him in just a flimsy pair of knickers and heels, she was trembling—almost as though they were about to make love for the first time.

It was ridiculous. She forced a laugh to break the mood; it didn't work.

'Something amusing?' he queried, sliding his hands beneath the elastic of her underpants and cupping her rear.

It jolted her into a state of hyperawareness. She shook her head but his lips were on hers, stalling any further movement.

It was a slow kiss—a kiss that deepened as his hands roamed her body, a kiss he didn't break even as he removed his hands to strip his own clothes away. He stepped out of his shoes, guiding Marnie towards the bed, all small movements, urgent movements, designed to bring them together as quickly as possible.

They'd kissed in her room before, but they had been different people then. He full of hope and certainty and she so willing to surrender herself to the feelings they shared.

He pushed the past away. It had haunted him long enough.

He was making love to his *wife*—not a figment of his memories. She was a red-blooded woman and she wanted him *now*.

His hands glided over her body, feeling every square inch, paving a way for his mouth to follow. His fingers pulled at her nipples while his lips teased the delicate flesh beneath her breasts, breathing warm air and making her back arch with desperate need. He dragged his mouth higher, running his teeth over her décolletage and then meeting her mouth once more.

There was so much he didn't understand about them—about himself. So much he would say if he knew how to find the words. Instead he kissed her with all the confusion he had become, the contradictions that now filled him.

'Nikos...' She groaned.

Did she understand?

Was this her way of telling him that she, too, was ready to let the past go? To lay those ghosts to rest once and for all?

'Please...'

A soft whisper. A sound of need that he would meet again and again for the rest of his life if he had the opportunity.

He entered her gently but she lifted herself higher, taking him deep and groaning as their bodies were unified once more.

Transfixed, he watched as she rode her first wave, her body quickly adjusting to his possession and welcoming him with giddy delight. He watched her fly high into the peaks of pleasure, so beautiful against this bed from her childhood.

And then he was joining her, his body meeting her questions, taking them, answering them, and cresting with her. Her fingers sought his and laced through them. He lifted their arms above her head, kissing away the pleasure-soaked moans that were becoming louder and more insistent. He absorbed them, but he was an echo chamber for them, for those same cries were deep inside him, too.

He felt her slowly quieten, and her body gradually stopped its fevered trembling so that only the sound of her husky breathing was left. He rolled onto the bed, bringing her with him, cradling her head against his chest. And he stayed like that, holding her, not wanting to speak—finding that he had nothing to say in any event—until her continued silence caused him to realise that she had fallen asleep.

He shifted a little so that he could look at her.

And guilt shot a hole in his heart.

It was Marnie—the Marnie he'd once loved and the Marnie he'd married. How could he think the past didn't matter? The past was a part of them. Her rejection had turned him into who he was. It had happened, but it was over with.

She was *his* Marnie.

His wife, his lover. Just Marnie.

Understanding was chased by bitter recrimination, as though he was waking from the depths of a nightmare.

His eyes slammed shut as acid filled his mouth. Because he'd *forced* her to marry him. He'd taken away any choice in the matter, skilfully applying just the right pressure to ensure she had no way of saying no.

And she'd risen to the challenge. She'd done what he'd asked of her. For her father? Or had there been a part of her that had wanted to see whatever it was they had been through to the bitter end?

The end.

He hadn't thought that far ahead. He lifted his finger and traced a line down her arm. In her sleep she smiled. It was a beautiful smile but it might as well have been a spoken accusation.

What the hell had he done? And why?

He lay there for hours, his mind spinning over the past, his body refusing to move from the closeness of hers. But eventually, somewhere after midnight, he gave up on sleep and shifted from the bed, taking care not to wake her. He dressed in a pair of boxers and a loose shirt before stepping quietly from the bedroom.

The house was in darkness, save for a few lamps placed through the hallway.

In the kitchen, midway through making coffee, he heard a noise and looked towards the door.

Whether Nikos or Anne Kenington was more surprised would have been difficult to say with certainty. Nikos flicked a glance at his wristwatch. Despite the lateness of the hour Anne was still wearing the same dress she'd been in at the party.

'Late night?' he murmured, inserting a pod into the machine.

Anne's smile was tight. 'And for you?'

He shrugged. 'I couldn't sleep.'

Anne expelled a sigh that could only be described as disapproving and moved farther into the kitchen. Closer, Nikos caught the smell of alcohol on her breath and realised her eyes were a little unfocussed.

'You're leaving tomorrow?' she asked.

He nodded. A shorter visit had seemed like a good idea, and nothing he'd seen since arriving had changed his mind. Except Marnie's smile. Out of nowhere he saw her as she'd been in the apple orchard, the sun glinting on her hair, a trickle of sugary fruit juice dribbling down her face, and his gut kicked. If anything, it served as vindication for how he'd handled Arthur's affairs. Her happiness here was no reason to remain longer.

'Such a short trip,' Anne murmured as she walked to the fridge and pulled out a bottle of wine.

Nikos watched as she reached into the cupboard and frowned, running her hands over an empty shelf before reaching lower and pulling out a Royal Doulton teacup. She sloshed Chardonnay into it, then placed the bottle on the bench.

'I'd thought you might be here a few days at least.'

His gaze was narrowed. 'Would you have liked us to stay longer?'

Her eyes met his and for a very brief moment he felt a surge of recognition. He'd adored Libby. She had been different from Marnie, but a beautiful person, and she'd faced her illness with such strength and humour. He saw that same resilience in Anne's eyes—and it surprised him to realise that they must have other similarities, too.

'I suppose not.' She laughed—a brittle sound that made him sad for her.

'Why?' he prompted, pulling his coffee cup from the machine and holding it in one hand.

'You're bad for my husband's blood pressure.'

Nikos laughed with true mirth. 'Am I?'

'He was in quite a mood this afternoon. Some birthday present...'

Curious, Nikos nodded. 'Did he tell you what we discussed?'

Anne's face was pinched. 'He gave me an indication,' she responded with cold civility. 'I suppose you think I should thank you?'

Another moment he'd thought he would relish. He shook his head, though, brushing her words away. 'It was no hardship for me to intervene.'

'I'm surprised you bothered,' she said quietly, imbibing more of her wine.

He shrugged. 'For Marnie...'

He let the rest of the sentence hang in the air, knowing he couldn't speak the bald-faced lie now. After all, it had all been for his own selfish gratification. None of this was really for his wife, was it?

'She loves you,' Anne said, her body so still she might have been carved from stone. 'She always has.'

He heard the words without allowing them to find any

credibility within him. 'She loved me six years ago, when you forced her to end it.'

Anne didn't visibly react. It was as though the past was a ribbon, pulling her backwards. 'She was miserable afterwards. I doubt she ever forgave us.'

It was a strange sense; he was both hot and cold. He didn't want to think of how Marnie had felt. He'd been so furious with her, so concerned with his own hurts, he'd never really given her situation any thought. She'd told him she'd been angry, though. Furious, she'd said. Had her fury matched his? It couldn't have or she would have held their course.

'She moved on,' he said quietly. 'Until recently.'

'But she didn't.'

Anne's eyes were darkened by guilt. She pushed up from the bench and strode a little way across the kitchen, then froze once more—a statue in the room.

'She continued to live and breathe, but that's not the same as moving on. She thought I didn't notice her reading about you in the papers. That I didn't catch her looking at photos of you.' She flicked her head over her shoulder, pinning him with a glance that spoke of true concern. 'She was so careful, but I saw the way she missed you. The way she seemed to wither for a long time. It was almost like losing two daughters.'

Disgust, anger and guilt at the way they had all failed Marnie gnawed through him.

Anne sipped her wine and moved back to her original spot, opposite Nikos. 'We introduced her to some lovely young men—'

'*Suitable* men?' he interjected, with a cynical strength to his words. But Anne's statement was slicing through him. The idea of Marnie having pined for him was one he couldn't contemplate.

'Yes, suitable men. Nice men.' She closed her eyes.

'She never mentioned your name, but I always knew you to be the reason it didn't work out. She never got over you.'

Nikos sipped his coffee but his mind was spinning back over their conversation in his office, when he'd first suggested they marry. She'd been so arctic. So cold!

But wasn't that Marnie's defence mechanism? Wasn't that how she behaved when her emotions were rioting all over the place? And her being a virgin? Was that simply because she'd never found someone who made her body tremble as it did for him? Had she chosen not to get serious with another guy because she still wanted *him*?

'I believed we were doing the right thing.' Anne's smile was tight. 'After Libby, we just wanted Marnie to be safe.'

'You thought I was somehow *unsafe*?' he barked, anger and frustration and impotence to change the past ravaging his temper.

'You *aren't* safe,' she responded sharply. 'The way she feels about you is a recipe for disaster.'

Marnie didn't still love him, did she? How could she after what he'd put her through? She might have loved him a year ago…even two months ago. But the way he'd burst back into her life had been the one thing that must have ruined any love between them.

He closed his eyes briefly.

Anne continued speaking, but she wasn't particularly focussed on her son-in-law. 'You must hate us. I know Marnie did for a long time. But I *love* her, Nikos. Everything I've done has been because I love her.'

'Yet you sought to control her life? You told her you would disinherit her if she didn't leave me?'

Anne winced as though he'd slapped her. 'Yes. Well, Arthur did…' A whisper. A hollow, tormented, grief-soaked admission. 'At the time I told myself that she must have known we were right. She broke up with you. And Marnie knew her own head and heart. If she'd *really* loved you, I told myself, she would have fought harder.'

Nikos felt a familiar sentiment echo within him.

'But she couldn't. We were holding on by a thread and Marnie knew that.'

'And what about Marnie?' he asked with dark anger, though he couldn't have said if it was directed at Anne, Arthur or himself.

'She was *Marnie*,' Anne said finally, drinking more wine with a small shrug. 'Determined to act as though everything was fine even if it was almost killing her.'

Nikos angled his head away, his dark eyes resting on their reflections in the window. Anne appeared smaller there, shrunken. Surprised, he looked at her and realised that the changes had taken place in real time—he just hadn't noticed them. She was smaller, wizened, stressed.

'How could you let her go through this?' he muttered, but his blame and recriminations were focussed on himself.

Anne pinned him with eyes that reminded him once more of Libby. 'Libby was such an easy child—so like me. I just understood her. But with Marnie... She's a puzzle I can't fathom.'

Nikos rubbed a hand across his jaw. 'Marnie is all that is good in the world,' he said finally. 'Often to her own detriment. She wants the best for those she loves, even when it means sacrificing her own happiness.'

Guilt over their marriage was a knife, deep in his gut.

'Yes!' Anne expelled an angry sigh. 'I love that girl, Nikos, but I don't always know *how* to love her. I suppose that sounds tremendously strange to you—she's my child, after all.'

His smile was thin. For Anne's words had lodged deep in his mind and begun to unravel with condemnation and acceptance. He had loved Marnie once, too, but never in the way she'd needed to be loved. His faults were on a par with Anne and Arthur Kenington's.

CHAPTER ELEVEN

MARNIE STOOD UNSTEADILY as the plane pitched yet again, rolled mercilessly by the thick cotton wool clouds that had clogged the entire journey from London to Athens.

Nikos, in the middle of a newspaper article, lifted his gaze curiously. He had been distracted for the entire flight, and he seemed almost to be rousing himself from a long way away now.

'Travel sickness,' she explained, moving quickly away from him towards the back of the plane.

She burst into the toilet, relieved to have made it just a second before losing the entire contents of her stomach. Her brow broke out in sweat and still she heaved, her whole body quivering with the exertion.

She moaned as the taste of metal filled her mouth and finally, spent, straightened. The mirror showed how unwell she'd been: the face that stared back at her was bright red, sweaty, and her eyes were slightly bloodshot in the corners.

She flushed the toilet and ran the cold water, washing her hands and splashing water over her face, enjoying the relief of the ice-cold liquid.

As a child she'd been prone to travel sickness. Even a short journey had brought on a spell of nausea. But it had been a long time since she'd felt it. Years. In fact the last time she'd been sick she'd been ten or eleven.

But what else could it be?

Marnie froze midway through patting her cheeks with a plush hand towel. Mentally she counted back the days to their wedding, her mind moving with an alacrity she wouldn't have thought it capable of a moment ago, while doubled over an aeroplane toilet.

They'd been married just over a month and they'd made love on their wedding night. And since that time a certain something had been glaringly absent.

She'd started the pill in plenty of time for it to have been effective. So what did that mean? Had going on birth control simply changed her normal cycle? Was that it? Or was she pregnant with Nikos's baby? Because what she was feeling felt altogether different, and a little terrifying.

The idea was a tiny seed she couldn't shake. It put roots down through her mind, so that by the time she returned to her seat, looking much more like her normal self, she was almost certain that she was indeed pregnant.

She'd need to do a test to be sure, but there was no room in her mind for doubt.

She barely spoke for the rest of the flight, and she was too caught up in her own imaginings to notice that Nikos was similarly silent. Brooding, even.

Athens was cool but humid when they landed; the clouds that had made their flight so bumpy were thick in the air, making the ground steam.

'I have some business to take care of,' Nikos murmured once they'd disembarked. His Ferrari was waiting on the Tarmac. 'I will need to go straight to my office once we're home.'

Marnie, secretly glad for this reprieve, time to ascertain whether or not she was in fact pregnant, nodded. 'Okay.'

It was all Marnie could do not to tell him of her suspicions as he drove the now familiar roads to his mansion.

But she wouldn't do that. Not until she knew for sure that there was a baby.

It would be a surprise—a shock, really.

But it didn't necessarily follow that it would be a nightmare, did it?

'A baby between us would never be magical and wonderful. It is the very last thing I would want.'

The words circled her mind.

She waited until he'd left, and then for Eléni to arrive, and somehow was casually able to ask for a ride to the markets to pick up some groceries.

The whole way there, making halting chitchat with Eléni, Marnie wondered what it would mean if she was actually, truly pregnant.

She paid for the groceries, stuffing the pregnancy test into her handbag rather than stowing it with the other shopping, and listened to Eléni the whole way home.

Finally she removed herself to her room to find out, once and for all, if her suspicions were right.

The test showed exactly what she had known it would.

Two bright blue lines.

She was pregnant.

With Nikos's baby.

Elation danced deep in her being. She felt its unmistakable warmth zing through her and she treasured it—because she knew that it would not last long. Complications would surely arise soon enough and take away the pleasure she felt.

For it was an incontrovertible truth that no matter what she chose to do she would be a part of Nikos's life for ever. And he of hers.

Where was her despair at that prospect? Her concern?

She looked into her heart and saw nothing—just joy.

Tears ran down her cheeks and for the first time in her

life they were happy tears. Tears that warmed her and
blessed her and made her feel as if she wanted to shout her
euphoria from the rooftops. It was not a simple joy—there
would be complications—but they paled in comparison to
the happiness that shone before her.

She needed to tell him—but not on the phone. She
would wait until he returned and leave him in no doubt
as to how pleased she was with this turn of events. Even
though she knew they had broken his cardinal rule...

The minutes of the day seemed to gang up on her, de-
ciding that they'd like to drag their way mutinously towards the hour of Nikos's arrival gleefully slowly rather
than with the alacrity she craved.

Just wondering when you'll be home?

She sent the message, her impatience burning through
her, fear threatening to take hold of her.

Not for a while. N.

Well, he'd be home eventually, and then she'd just have
to put her hope in his hands and pray he didn't crush it.

The first sign that there was a problem was that Nikos
didn't drive himself home. A luxurious limousine pulled
up out at the front and Marnie, hovering in her office with
its view of the driveway, wondered briefly if they had unexpected company.

When Nikos emerged from the back his large frame
seemed different. Slightly unsteady. He stood for a moment, a hand braced on the roof of the car, his eyes scanning the front of his house. Why did he look so grim? Had
something happened?

Concerned, she moved quickly through the house,
reaching the front door at the same time he did. She heard

his keys drop to the ground outside and pulled the door inwards, her expression perplexed.

Until she smelled the Scotch and realised that her husband—the father of her tiny, tiny baby—had obviously been drinking. Heavily.

'Nik…?' she said with disbelief, holding the door wide and letting him in.

Marnie had never seen him anything other than in complete control. She was struggling to make sense of what might have happened in the hours since they'd returned from London to lead him to be in this state.

'My wife,' he said, as though it brought him little pleasure.

Confusion thick in her mind, she waited for him to move deeper into the house so she could close the door. 'Have you been out?'

'No,' he muttered. 'I have been in my office.'

Unconsciously, she moved a hand to her stomach. 'Drinking?'

He expelled an angry breath. 'Apparently.'

Marnie nodded, but he still wasn't making sense. The uncharacteristic act jarred with everything she knew about this man. He was a disciplined control freak.

Out of nowhere old jealousies and suspicions erupted. 'Alone?'

His eyes narrowed, but he nodded.

'Why?' she asked finally, putting a hand on his elbow in order to guide him towards the kitchen.

But he pulled away, walking determinedly ahead of her, his physical ability apparently not as affected as she'd first thought.

She walked behind him, and once in the kitchen moved to the fridge. As if on autopilot, she pulled out the ingredients for a toasted cheese sandwich, her eyes flicking to him every few moments. And he stared at her. He stared at her with an intensity that filled her body with fire and flame even as she was laced with confusion and anxiety.

So telling him about the baby wasn't going to happen, she admitted to herself. At least not until the following day, when he might be in a headspace to comprehend what she was saying.

'*Why*, Marnie?' He repeated her question in a tone that was so like the way he'd spoken in the past it made her chest heavy; his words seemed to ring with disdain and dislike.

She tried not to let it fill her heart but it was there. Doubt. Hurt. Aching sadness.

'What's wrong?' she said finally. 'Has something happened?'

He reached into his pocket and pulled out an envelope. 'Your mother believes you've spent the last six years pining for me. That you have loved me this whole time.'

Marnie started, her eyes flying to his involuntarily. Her mouth was dry. 'I…I don't understand why that matters. What my mother says…how I felt. What difference does it make right now to this marriage?'

He spoke slowly, his tone emphatic. 'Did you stay single and celibate because you love me?'

Marnie's heart dropped.

She spun away from him but Nikos raised his voice.

'Damn it, Marnie. You broke up with me. You walked away from us.'

'I know,' she whispered, tears springing to her eyes. The happiness of the last twenty-four hours was being swallowed by old hurts. 'I thought we agreed we wouldn't talk about the past any more?'

He slammed his palm against the benchtop. 'Why didn't you come back? Why didn't you call me when you realised you were still in love with me?'

'You'd moved on,' she said simply. 'And nothing had changed for me.'

'You were so emphatic when you ended it. You convinced me you didn't care for me, that you had never been serious. You completely echoed your father's feelings about me and men of my *upbringing*.' He spat the word like a curse.

She recoiled as though he'd slapped her. 'I *had* to do that! You wouldn't have accepted it unless I made sure you truly believed it was over.' She shook her head and no longer bothered to check the tears that stung her eyes. 'I hated saying those things to you when it was the opposite of how I felt.'

He was not his usual self, but even on a bad day and after a fair measure of Scotch Nikos was better than anyone at debating and reasoning.

He honed his thoughts quickly back to the point at hand. 'You admit you've loved me this whole time?'

Marnie froze, her only movement the rapid rise and fall of her chest as she tried to draw breath into her lungs. She felt that she'd been caught—not in a lie so much as in the truth.

'I would never have done this if I'd known,' he said after a beat of silence had passed—one he took for her acquiescence.

'Done what?' She didn't look at him. Her voice was a whisper into the room.

'This marriage…'

Her heart fell as if from a great height. It was pulverised at her feet, a tangling mass of heaving hopes.

'It was the worst kind of wrong to use you like this.'

She couldn't stifle her sob. 'Is that what you were doing?' She forced herself to look at him—and then wished she hadn't when the intensity of his expression left her short of breath.

He spoke with a cold detachment that was so much worse than the heat of an argument. 'I forced you to marry me. Just as your parents forced you to leave me. I am no better than them. Hell, I consider my crimes to be considerably greater.'

He pushed the back of the envelope open and lifted a piece of paper out. One page. When he handed it to her it was still warm from having been nestled close to his chest all afternoon.

'But at least I can atone for my sins.'

'What's this?' she asked, even as her eyes dropped to the page.

'*Petition for Divorce*' was typed neatly across the top, and as she skimmed lower she saw her name written beside Nikos's. He'd already signed his name. A masculine scrawl of hard intent.

Marnie was still. So still. Briefly she wondered if she might pass out. She felt hot and cold, as she'd done on the flight. She dropped the page and moved backwards until her bottom connected with the bench. She stayed there, glad for the support. Her head was spinning.

'Divorce?'

'I was wrong.' The words were saturated with bleak despair. He was begging her to understand. 'I regret everything I said to you that day in my office. I heard your father was going bankrupt and this idea came to me. I acted on it before I could realise what a stupid mistake it was. I need to undo it.'

She stared at him in shock. 'You can't simply *undo* a marriage. You can't undo what we are!'

'This piece of paper would suggest otherwise,' he said, with a factual determination that left her cold.

'Nikos!' His name was a plea. She looked at the paper. 'Do you want me to leave?'

'I don't want you to stay,' he said thickly. 'Not like this.'

Marnie dropped her head forward. Tears splashed out of her eyes.

'I've had the pre-nuptial agreement voided,' he murmured. 'And you need never worry that your father's finances will be in trouble—'

He thought of the other provisions he'd had enabled, but dismissed the need to discuss them at that point. Actually, he doubted he had the mental wherewithal in that moment to do justice to any of the financial arrangements he'd put in place.

'Listen to me,' she interrupted, her voice unsteady, her tone showing urgency. 'My father has nothing to do with this.'

'He *is* why we married.'

But it was almost a question, a demand for information.

His eyes locked to hers in a way that stole Marnie's breath. It was time to tell him the truth. She didn't believe she'd married for love necessarily, and yet hadn't it always been there? Even when she was furious, wasn't it because she loved him so much and felt so hurt by his actions?

But at that moment her courage was thin on the ground. She tried a different approach, desperately needing to understand what was going on.

'Why don't you tell me what's happened? Last night was fine. Last night was amazing. We danced and spoke as though…as though…we were making progress,' she finished lamely. 'We made love,' she said—an anguished reminder of the beautiful way he'd taken her. It *had* been making love—not just sex, but perfect, intimate love.

'You need to leave me,' he said quietly, taking a step backwards. 'Let me be as clear tonight as you were six years ago, when you ended things the first time. For both our sakes, please leave. Our marriage was a mistake. I should have known better than to even contemplate it.

Now you must go. It is over between us and you should be grateful for that.'

She watched as he strode out of the kitchen in what she considered to be the middle of their argument, and was torn between chasing after him and doing just as he'd said. How easy it would be to numbly pack a suitcase and go— to leave this minefield for the peace of solitude.

Only what followed wouldn't be easy. Leaving him once had hurt like hell and she'd never recovered. And the way she'd felt then was a fraction of what she felt now. She'd lived with him, and beyond that she'd committed her full self to this man and their marriage.

But could she keep trying to make their marriage work if he didn't even *want* the marriage any more? She stared at the piece of paper, anger building brick by brick inside her.

When had her mother and her husband had this *tête-à-tête*? And if Anne knew how badly Marnie had longed for Nikos why hadn't she talked to Marnie about it? Why hadn't she taken back the edict that had led to Marnie ruining her relationship with the only man she'd ever loved?

She caught a scream in her mouth; just a muted sound of frustration erupted into the silent kitchen. She had been pulled in a thousand directions by those she most cared about and now fury was building within her.

She stormed across the room, her feet planted heavily on the tiles, until she reached the sliding glass doors. She pushed them open and went outside. At the pool, she ripped her dress over her head, then leapt in. The water was a balm to her fraught senses and it absorbed the stinging, angry tears that were running freely down her cheeks.

Divorce?

After a month?

When she was pregnant with his baby?

And completely in love with him?

And he loved *her*, didn't he? She was almost sure of it. So why tell her to leave, then? None of it made sense.

But she wasn't going to let history repeat itself. She loved him more than ever before, and that meant staying to fight—not running away.

When Nikos awoke the next morning it was still dark and he was alone in his bed. He sat up, intent on going for his usual run, but a blinding headache shattered his temples.

And then it all came flooding back to him.

His conversation with Anne Kenington... *'I love her. I just don't know* how *to love her.'*

The divorce papers that had seemed like such an inspired idea at his lowest ebb.

Marnie's face as she'd stared at him, tears on her lashes, her slender body shaking as she comprehended his words.

'I want you to go. It is over between us.'

He squeezed his eyes shut, but that only enabled him to remember more clearly. The pain had slammed into her like a wall. Her harsh reaction to his simple solution. His belief that by divorcing her he could erase the barbarism of his behaviour.

He swore loudly and stood, ignoring the blinding pain that spiked in his brain. *Marnie.* Where was she? Had she left?

A cursory inspection of their room showed that her clothes were all in their usual spot. Relief was brief. She hadn't gone anywhere. *Had she?* He moved into their *en-suite* bathroom intent on making himself look slightly more civilised before facing the music.

It smelled of her. Lavender, violets...feminine and sweet. His gut clenched and he swore again.

He showered quickly and wrapped a towel around his waist while brushing his teeth. The toothpaste tube was empty and he tossed it carelessly in the rubbish bin. It missed. When he crouched down to retrieve it, his head complaining the whole time, something unusual caught his eye. A box.

He lifted it out and stared at it in confusion.

A pregnancy test?

That didn't make any sense.

Marnie was on the pill. But it sure as hell wasn't Eléni's. Which meant that somehow, for some reason, Marnie had had reason to believe she might be pregnant. He opened the box but it was empty. Nor was there a test in the trash.

With renewed urgency he pulled on a pair of shorts and shirt and practically ran out of the room and through the house. There were several guest rooms but they were all empty. Fear was building.

What if she *was* pregnant? Would he still be strong enough to let her go? If she chose to divorce him—hell, she might have already signed the damned papers—would he let the divorce proceed?

And what if she stayed with him because of the baby? Could he live with her knowing he'd trapped her—twice—into marriage?

He checked her office. It was empty, neat.

Then his own office—empty.

Finally, he went to the kitchen.

And there she was.

Marnie.

Sitting on the sofa, staring out at the lifting sun, her face pale, her eyes a terrifying maelstrom of feelings and fears.

What could he say to her? What right did he have to explain?

He walked quietly and then crouched in front of her, directly in Marnie's line of sight.

'Have you slept?'

She blinked her eyes at him and then looked away, over

his shoulder, focussing on the colours smudged across the sky. 'I didn't leave.'

A muscle jerked at his temple. 'I'm glad.'

Her eyes flew to his again. Confusion. Hurt. 'Why?'

She reminded him of a wounded animal. He swore under his breath and dragged a hand through his hair. He needed to reassure her. To explain. She deserved at least that much. But his own questions were burning through him.

For a man like Nikos, not knowing what to say or how to negotiate on the terms of his marriage brought with it great frustration. He was used to commanding a room. He had not doubted his ability to bring people to his way of thinking for a very long time.

Business, though, was predictable—easy for a man like Nikos. He would discover what motivated a person and exploit that to gain his own success.

Marnie was motivated by love.

Loyalty.

Affection and faithfulness.

And he didn't want her to be with him for any of those reasons but one.

'You gave me divorce papers last night.' Her eyes had an unexpected strength in them. 'Why?'

He expelled a breath. 'Isn't that obvious?'

'You don't want to be married to me,' she whispered, the words a ghost of sentiment in the large room.

'I don't want you to feel *forced* to stay married to me,' he clarified.

She nodded, her gaze refusing to meet his. If only he *had* pushed her away! She'd ended up falling as much in love with him as ever, and now it was so much worse—for she'd tasted the mind-blowing bliss that came from sharing his bed and his life.

'You were happy to give me an ultimatum at one time. What's changed?'

Did he detect the note of challenge in her voice?

His smile was lacking any true happiness. 'We are married, but you are not my wife.' He stood, his back straight, his shoulders square. 'It turns out you can't really force someone into a marriage.'

'Isn't that what's happened here?'

He shook his head. 'I believed that having you as my wife would make you mine. It doesn't work like that, though.' His expression was bleak for a moment, before hard certainty crossed it. 'You will never be able to forget the way I propositioned you, and nor will I. I look at you and see the man I have become. A man I despise.'

'You have helped my father,' she said quietly. 'I could never hate you after what you've done for him.'

'You have to release us both from this. I can't live with how I've hurt you.'

She nodded, her throat raw from unshed tears. 'You *have* hurt me,' she whispered. 'Just as I hurt you. Does that make us even now?'

He stood up, moving angrily towards the glass doors and staring out. 'You were a teenager. A *grieving* teenager. You hurt my pride and my ego and I left. I should have stayed. It takes courage to stay and fight for what you want. But I didn't like how it felt to be rejected, so I went off like a sulking child.' He thrust his hands in his pockets. 'I didn't deserve you.'

She lifted her feet onto the sofa so she could rest her chin against her knees. 'Fighting would have been pointless. You would have only upset me more than I already was. I truly believed I had no choice but to end it.'

He nodded, thinking of the pregnancy test box he'd discovered. He turned slowly, but pain was a fresh wave crashing over him. She was a contradiction of fragility and strength. Broken but resolved. Determined and disappointed.

He strode to her, a guttural sound of angst tearing from his chest. '*I* have broken whatever we used to be—not you. If you are pregnant I will support you. I will make sure you have everything you and the baby need. But I will not let you use that as a reason to stay with me.'

Shock flashed over Marnie and her skin paled to paper-white. 'The...baby?' She swallowed. 'How did you know?' What was the point in denying it?

'I found the box in our bathroom,' he responded, so close he could touch her, but not allowing himself to do so.

She hadn't bothered to hide it because she'd thought they would have a perfect dinner together, over which she would share with him the happy news. *Happy news!* Well, at least there was still some truth in that. Thoughts of the baby filled her shattered heart with a slight antiseptic against the pain.

'Is it true?' he asked, his words anguished.

Slowly she nodded, pulling her lower lip between her teeth. 'Yes...'

'*Thee mou!*' He groaned, standing and running a hand over his eyes. He seemed to stand there for ever, a heaving man, his whole body showing instant rejection of the idea of their child. Just as he'd said he would.

What had she expected? That he would welcome this news?

'I am so sorry.' He groaned again, dropping his hand and pinning her with the full force of his shocked gaze.

'Sorry?' she repeated, feeling numbed now, so fresh pain wasn't capable of sinking in.

'First I trapped you with blackmail and now you must feel trapped by our baby. But you can leave. You *must* leave. A baby is no reason to continue this farce.'

She sobbed and nodded. 'I know that.'

Neither spoke for a long time. Marnie was trying to imagine a life without Nikos and all she saw was the bleakness that had been her bedfellow for these past six years.

'If I could fix this, I would,' he said.

She nodded again, resting her cheek on her knees. She had chosen to stay and fight, but so far she had done a lot of listening and no actual fighting. She tried to find the strength in her heart, but it was in ruins.

'There is something else you should know.' He spoke with a grim finality to his words. 'I could not find the words to explain last night.'

'Explain what?' she whispered, wondering at the pain in her throat.

'I have bought Kenington Hall and put it in your name.'

She lifted her head sharply, almost giving herself whiplash in the process. Everything else disappeared from her mind. 'You've *what*?'

He expelled a sigh and crouched down on his haunches so that their eyes were level. 'You love the property, and I wanted you to know it to be safe. That no matter what happened to your father, or to our marriage, you would have the security of your family home.'

She let that statement sink in. 'When did you do this?'

'When I met with your father.'

She nodded, but nothing was making sense. 'Were you planning to divorce me even then? Was it to be my consolation prize?' Grief lanced her. 'What did I do wrong? I thought we were making this work...'

'You did nothing wrong, Marnie, except fall in love with an arrogant, selfish bastard like me.' He dropped his head into his hands. 'I didn't buy the house because I wanted to leave you. I bought it because I wanted you to understand that you have options. That you and your family are safe. Even before speaking with your mother I knew I had to give you back your freedom before I could even hope to make amends.'

'I have never considered myself to lack freedom,' she inserted seriously, her eyes sparkling, her mind moving quickly. 'So you *did* want to make this marriage a real one?'

A muscle jerked in his jaw. 'I cannot say if I ever thought of it in those terms.'

He dared to lift a hand and touch her soft hair. Fear at what he was on the brink of losing was all around him—a pit of despair he knew would swallow him if he didn't explain himself better than he was doing now.

'I knew only that I wanted you to look at me with the love you once felt. That I wanted to be able to smile at you with the love that is in *here*.' He tapped his hand against his chest.

Marnie made a sound of disbelief.

'You *should* leave me. You can go and it will not change how I feel about you. Your father is out of debt. Kenington Hall is safe in your hands. And I will be as involved as you allow me to be in our child's life. You must decide what will make you happy.'

Happy? That felt so far away.

She stood up, something snapping inside her. She could no longer sit still as though this were a normal discussion. Her temper flared. She spun round, her hands on her hips, her face showing the full extent of her rage. There was nothing remotely cold about her now. She was all feelings and flame.

'You're such an *idiot*!' she shouted at the top of her lungs. 'I have *always* loved you! Always! Even when I thought I was over you, how could I be? I married you! And—newsflash!—I didn't *have* to! Even to save my father's financial situation. I would only ever have married one man on earth. *You.* Only you.'

She wrapped her arms around herself.

'You were right before, when you said that you should have stayed and fought for what we were. I don't think it would have made a difference, but it's what you *do* when you're in love with someone. You don't bloody walk away. I'm not going to walk away now, because I love you—even when you're almost impossible to comprehend.'

He stared at her, but his expression was blank, as though her words were a problem he had to decode.

'I was furious with you when we got married. *Livid.* What a stupid thing you did, blackmailing me like this! But I still loved you. Every night of this marriage has been like slowly unwrapping a present, piece by piece, getting to find my way back to you—'

'I have pushed you away,' he interrupted, arguing the sense of her statement.

'Yes, you have—but you've also pulled me close. So close that I've been inside your soul. You've let me in. And you *dare* turn up with divorce papers, as though our marriage is a simple contract you can dissolve? You *dare* relegate our love to an agreement that you alone can end?'

Startled by her anger, he stood, wishing to placate her. He put an arm on her shoulder but she jerked away.

'No!' she snapped. 'I'm not finished yet.'

Her eyes held a warning and, fascinated, he was silent.

'You have been hitting me over the head with the fact that I flicked a switch and walked away from you six years ago. I didn't. I didn't flick a switch. I made the worst mistake of my life when I left you, and I'm not going to do it again.' She straightened her shoulders. 'If you want to divorce me—if you don't want me any more—then tell me that. You can make that decision. But don't tell me that leaving you is in my best interests—because I know what life is like without you and there is no life on earth that I want more than *this* life, here—right here with you.'

His breath was ragged, torn from his lungs. 'How can you feel that?' he murmured with a growing sense of wonderment. 'I have been—'

'You have been Nikos.' She cut across him, but softly, kindly, with the compassion that was always so close to her surface. 'Determined, arrogant and good.' She moved closer. 'Do you think either of us really understood what we were doing and why? You wanted to help my family. I believe that was at the heart of everything you did.'

He made a sound and shook his head, but she lifted a finger to his lips.

'Whatever motivated you to blackmail me into this marriage, I will never resent you for it. How can I? I've missed you and now I have you.' She paused, her eyes scanning his. 'I *do* have you, don't I?'

He wrapped his arms around her waist, crushing her to him. 'You have all of me, for all time.' The words were a promise against her cheek. '*All* of me. And you are the best of me.'

She shut her eyes and listened to the pounding of his heart. Her lips twitched in a smile that shone with true happiness.

Gradually Nikos pulled backwards, dropping a hand to her flat stomach. 'A baby was not on our agenda,' he said, as if just comprehending the reality of their situation.

'Apparently the baby had other ideas. I dare say it has a lot of your determination.'

He laughed. 'Let us hope that is balanced by your warmth and kindness.'

'Well, I guess we'll find out in about eight months.'

'And you are truly happy?'

'Nikos!' She laughed shakily. 'When I found out I was pregnant I wanted to shout it from the rooftops. I know it wasn't meant to be part of the plan, but it felt so *right*.'

He frowned, wondering how long she'd shouldered this secret. 'When did you first suspect?'

She smiled. 'Not until we were on the plane back to Greece.'

'And then I told you to leave me.' His face paled with remembered regrets. 'It was for *you*, Marnie. I didn't *want* you to go. You know this to be true?'

She nodded. 'I've never seen you like that.'

His smile was grim. 'I have only ever drunk to excess one other time in my life—the night your father paid me off and I took his money. Then, too, I felt like a shadow of the man I wanted to be.'

'Don't say that,' she murmured, resting her head against his chest. She stood there quietly for a moment. 'My father wouldn't have liked selling you the house...'

He breathed in her sweet fragrance and a sense of deep gratitude filled him. To think that he'd almost pushed her away for good! He would never make that mistake again. Not in his life.

'He...understood the necessity of it,' Nikos said after a moment. '*Agape mou*, I thought I would relish that moment. I had fantasised about seeing your father a broken man. I had dreamed of being in a position to throw my own success and wealth in his face and see him suffer. But at the first opportunity to do so I saw only you. I saw you and discovered that loving you meant loving *all* of you. Even your family. If you married me because you love me then you must understand that I have helped Arthur because I love you. It was not a payment for your marrying me.'

The words filled her with love and certainty—certainty that they were right where they should be. Together.

But she pulled a face of mock consideration. 'Well, it seems to me, then, that you haven't upheld your end of the deal.'

Sensing the amusement in her words, he answered in

kind. 'I suppose you're right. Is there something else I can offer instead?'

She pressed a finger to her chin and pretended to consider it. 'I can think of a few things…'

He surprised her by scooping her up and laying her down on the sofa. His mouth sought hers and he tasted her giddy delight there and answered it.

'Starting with right now?'

'I will expect the payment terms to be over a very long time,' she said, pushing at his shorts.

'Would the rest of our lives do?'

She sighed, her body firing with insatiable need for her husband. 'It just might.'

EPILOGUE

One year later

IT WAS THE ice sculpture that was the final straw.

She shook her head, torn between feeling cross and amused as she tore through the villa in search of her husband.

She found him by the pool, hands on hips, eyes staring out at the ocean. They'd been married for almost a year, and still the sight of him could stop her in her tracks. Her heart hammered roughly against her ribs, beating wildly as she approached him.

'A *swan*?' she said from just behind his shoulder, her expression one of utter disbelief. 'Seriously?'

His grin as he turned around skittled any discontent she had felt over his lavish decorations.

'It's summer,' she pointed out with a shake of her head, but her grumble was somewhat faint-hearted.

'Almost autumn.'

'Almost,' she responded archly. 'And it's as hot as Hades today. That thing's going to be iced water before anyone gets here.'

'So we will drink it!' He laughed. 'How many times does our daughter get christened?' he said, with such impeccable logic that all her objections were silenced.

'You're right.' Marnie smiled up at him, giving in to

temptation and wrapping her arms around his waist. 'And now I have another bone to pick with you.'

'Oh?' he murmured, his lips still pressed to hers.

She straightened, trying to be businesslike. 'The trust just called me to report that a rather sizeable donation has been made in Lulu's name.'

His smile lit the world on fire—starting with Marnie's heart. She was scorched with happiness.

'What else can I give you and our daughter on her christening? You will not let me buy you jewels or clothes... you insist she has all she needs. But this, I think, you *will* let me do.'

Marnie nodded, tears of happiness clogging her throat. 'But it's so much...'

'For a cause that means the world to you—and therefore to me. I still remember what you said to me, *agape mou*. That one day, through your efforts and the efforts of people like you, young girls like Libby might not get sick any more.'

He pressed a finger beneath Marnie's chin, lifting her eyes to meet his. She felt the love and commitment that underscored every decision he made.

'We have our own little girl now. How can you doubt my desire to work with you on this?'

Love coiled inside her. 'Thank you.' Her voice was husky. Emotions were too strong to contain. She lifted up on tiptoe and pressed a kiss to his lips. 'Why did we invite all these people over?'

He kissed her hungrily, his tongue exploring her mouth, his hands holding her tight against his body.

But for only a moment.

Then he lifted himself away, grinning as if he *hadn't* been shaken to the core by their molten hot connection.

'To see my ice sculpture,' he said, and laughed.

She rolled her eyes, but her mind was drifting. 'If only we had an extra hour...'

He grimaced, looking past her shoulder. 'If only we had an extra ten minutes...'

He saw their guests through the glass doors and kissed the top of her head.

'I will make you a promise,' he said in an undertone.

Marnie nodded. 'Oh, yes? I'm all ears, Mr Kyriazis.'

'Not from where I am standing.' He grinned at her, his handsome face a collection of lines and shapes that formed an inimitable image of masculinity.

Playfully, Marnie punched his upper arm. 'I believe you were making me a promise?'

'Soon we will be alone in our home again, and then I will show you just what that dress and you are making me want.'

Her pulse was lurching out of control. She lifted herself up on tiptoe again and kissed his lips, smiling as familiar sensations rocked her to her core.

'You'd better,' she said simply.

He wrapped an arm around her shoulder, pulling her to his side and knowing how right it was that they should be together. Everything in his world seemed to shine with the perfection that Marnie brought to his life.

'Your parents are here,' he murmured, looking down into the villa as Anne and Arthur Kenington made their way through the house.

Marnie took a moment to observe them, staying right where she was. Anne was her usual self—elegant and perfectly neat, despite the fact they'd come straight from the airport. Although a flight in Nikos's jet was hardly an arduous ordeal. Arthur Kenington showed the greatest change. He was dressed casually in a pale polo shirt and a pair of beige chinos. His hair was a little longer, and there were more lines on his face now—lines Marnie chose to believe were formed by happiness.

'Darling, there's a puddle forming in the foyer,' Anne said with pursed lips as she swept onto the terrace.

A breeze lifted past them, drawing with it the tang of the ocean and the sweetness of Libby's rose garden. Marnie inhaled, drawing strength from this reminder of her sister before steeling herself to enjoy the next few hours. Her parents were not perfect, but they were still her parents. And, fortunately for Marnie, despite their meddling and strong opinions she and Nikos had found their way together in the end.

'That would be the ice sculpture.' Marnie winked up at her husband, then moved towards her mother, kissing her cheek. She hugged her dad before returning to Nikos's side. 'Thanks for coming.'

'Of course.' Anne nodded. 'Where is our granddaughter?'

'She's with her uncle.' Marnie grinned. 'Her honorary uncle.'

Anderson emerged at that moment, their chubby dark-haired little girl propped on one hip.

'Nothing honourable about *him*,' Nikos teased, with a genuine smile reserved for their closest friend. 'Unlike you, Lady Heiress.'

She shook her head, her hands extended for the baby Elizabeth. But Lulu only had eyes for her father.

Marnie laughed. 'I see!' She shook her head. 'That's the way it's going to be, huh?'

'It is because I am not often here when she is awake.'

'Sure it is,' Marnie said with another laugh. 'And also because you spoil her silly. That's okay—I'm not offended.'

And she wasn't. How could she be? She had everything she'd ever wanted in life.

It was a beautiful afternoon, filled with happiness and

joy. Finally, though, after the last of the guests had left and Lulu was fast asleep, Marnie went in search of her husband.

She found him on the terrace, his eyes focussed contemplatively on the shimmering moon. It was a cool night now, and Marnie wrapped her arms around herself for warmth.

Nikos noticed—as he did everything about his wife—and shrugged out of his jacket, placing it around her slender shoulders on instinct.

'Here, *agape mou*,' he said, pulling her closer to his warmth.

'Thank you,' she murmured, inhaling his intoxicatingly masculine scent. 'Have I ever told you there was a time when I hated you calling me that?' she asked softly.

'Did you?'

'It just reminded me of what I wanted from you. What I doubted you'd ever feel for me.'

Her eyes pierced his, and for a second those thoughts and feelings were right there before her. Such pain and heartbreak! How had that ever been their story when there was now such love between them? Such joy and trust?

She blinked to clear those dark vestiges of the past.

'Did you doubt, Mrs Kyriazis? Did you really doubt?'

His eyes held hers, and in them she saw the truth that perhaps she'd always held deep in her heart. The incontrovertibility of who they were to one another.

His soft sigh breathed warmth across her temple. 'I called you that, even when we were at odds, because I needed to believe we could be that to one another again. I wanted to feel that I had the right...'

Her smile shifted her features, taking his breath away completely.

'It sounds a little like *you* were the one who doubted we'd find our way here.'

He put an arm around her waist, his fingers feathering

over her hip. 'Not for a second.' His voice was gravelly. 'I could never accept a world without you in it.'

'Even if that meant blackmailing me?' she teased, finding it almost impossible to credit the start of their marriage with the state of it now.

'Even then.' He dropped a kiss against her hair. 'Will you ever forgive me for that?'

'Forgive you? Hmm...' She pretended to think, her eyes full of love and amusement. 'I can think of one way you could make it up to me.'

He smiled softly. 'Your wish is my command. Although in this case I think it is my wish also.'

The stars shone overhead and the rose garden was bathed with magical milky moonlight. Nikos Kyriazis kissed his wife, carrying her into their now quiet home.

And it *was* a home. Not simply a house, as it had been for so long.

Now it was a collection of walls that contained their family's life, that was filled with pictures and love and the kind of warmth he had only ever dreamed possible. It was a home he shared with Marnie and Lulu, just as he shared his heart and his being with them.

A man who had never known love was now overflowing with it, and always would be.

* * * * *

Look out for more Clare Connelly titles
—coming soon!

MILLS & BOON®
Hardback – August 2017

ROMANCE

An Heir Made in the Marriage Bed	Anne Mather
The Prince's Stolen Virgin	Maisey Yates
Protecting His Defiant Innocent	Michelle Smart
Pregnant at Acosta's Demand	Maya Blake
The Secret He Must Claim	Chantelle Shaw
Carrying the Spaniard's Child	Jennie Lucas
A Ring for the Greek's Baby	Melanie Milburne
Bought for the Billionaire's Revenge	Clare Connelly
The Runaway Bride and the Billionaire	Kate Hardy
The Boss's Fake Fiancée	Susan Meier
The Millionaire's Redemption	Therese Beharrie
Captivated by the Enigmatic Tycoon	Bella Bucannon
Tempted by the Bridesmaid	Annie O'Neil
Claiming His Pregnant Princess	Annie O'Neil
A Miracle for the Baby Doctor	Meredith Webber
Stolen Kisses with Her Boss	Susan Carlisle
Encounter with a Commanding Officer	Charlotte Hawkes
Rebel Doc on Her Doorstep	Lucy Ryder
The CEO's Nanny Affair	Joss Wood
Tempted by the Wrong Twin	Rachel Bailey

MILLS & BOON®
Large Print – August 2017

ROMANCE

The Italian's One-Night Baby — Lynne Graham
The Desert King's Captive Bride — Annie West
Once a Moretti Wife — Michelle Smart
The Boss's Nine-Month Negotiation — Maya Blake
The Secret Heir of Alazar — Kate Hewitt
Crowned for the Drakon Legacy — Tara Pammi
His Mistress with Two Secrets — Dani Collins
Stranded with the Secret Billionaire — Marion Lennox
Reunited by a Baby Bombshell — Barbara Hannay
The Spanish Tycoon's Takeover — Michelle Douglas
Miss Prim and the Maverick Millionaire — Nina Singh

HISTORICAL

Claiming His Desert Princess — Marguerite Kaye
Bound by Their Secret Passion — Diane Gaston
The Wallflower Duchess — Liz Tyner
Captive of the Viking — Juliet Landon
The Spaniard's Innocent Maiden — Greta Gilbert

MEDICAL

Their Meant-to-Be Baby — Caroline Anderson
A Mummy for His Baby — Molly Evans
Rafael's One Night Bombshell — Tina Beckett
Dante's Shock Proposal — Amalie Berlin
A Forever Family for the Army Doc — Meredith Webber
The Nurse and the Single Dad — Dianne Drake

MILLS & BOON®
Hardback – September 2017

ROMANCE

The Tycoon's Outrageous Proposal	Miranda Lee
Cipriani's Innocent Captive	Cathy Williams
Claiming His One-Night Baby	Michelle Smart
At the Ruthless Billionaire's Command	Carole Mortimer
Engaged for Her Enemy's Heir	Kate Hewitt
His Drakon Runaway Bride	Tara Pammi
The Throne He Must Take	Chantelle Shaw
The Italian's Virgin Acquisition	Michelle Conder
A Proposal from the Crown Prince	Jessica Gilmore
Sarah and the Secret Sheikh	Michelle Douglas
Conveniently Engaged to the Boss	Ellie Darkins
Her New York Billionaire	Andrea Bolter
The Doctor's Forbidden Temptation	Tina Beckett
From Passion to Pregnancy	Tina Beckett
The Midwife's Longed-For Baby	Caroline Anderson
One Night That Changed Her Life	Emily Forbes
The Prince's Cinderella Bride	Amalie Berlin
Bride for the Single Dad	Jennifer Taylor
A Family for the Billionaire	Dani Wade
Taking Home the Tycoon	Catherine Mann

0817 GEN STD HB

MILLS & BOON®
Large Print – September 2017

ROMANCE

The Sheikh's Bought Wife	Sharon Kendrick
The Innocent's Shameful Secret	Sara Craven
The Magnate's Tempestuous Marriage	Miranda Lee
The Forced Bride of Alazar	Kate Hewitt
Bound by the Sultan's Baby	Carol Marinelli
Blackmailed Down the Aisle	Louise Fuller
Di Marcello's Secret Son	Rachael Thomas
Conveniently Wed to the Greek	Kandy Shepherd
His Shy Cinderella	Kate Hardy
Falling for the Rebel Princess	Ellie Darkins
Claimed by the Wealthy Magnate	Nina Milne

HISTORICAL

The Secret Marriage Pact	Georgie Lee
A Warriner to Protect Her	Virginia Heath
Claiming His Defiant Miss	Bronwyn Scott
Rumours at Court (Rumors at Court)	Blythe Gifford
The Duke's Unexpected Bride	Lara Temple

MEDICAL

Their Secret Royal Baby	Carol Marinelli
Her Hot Highland Doc	Annie O'Neil
His Pregnant Royal Bride	Amy Ruttan
Baby Surprise for the Doctor Prince	Robin Gianna
Resisting Her Army Doc Rival	Sue MacKay
A Month to Marry the Midwife	Fiona McArthur

MILLS & BOON®

Why shop at millsandboon.co.uk?

Each year, thousands of romance readers find their perfect read at millsandboon.co.uk. That's because we're passionate about bringing you the very best romantic fiction. Here are some of the advantages of shopping at www.millsandboon.co.uk:

* **Get new books first**—you'll be able to buy your favourite books one month before they hit the shops

* **Get exclusive discounts**—you'll also be able to buy our specially created monthly collections, with up to 50% off the RRP

* **Find your favourite authors**—latest news, interviews and new releases for all your favourite authors and series on our website, plus ideas for what to try next

* **Join in**—once you've bought your favourite books, don't forget to register with us to rate, review and join in the discussions

Visit **www.millsandboon.co.uk**
for all this and more today!